Northern Plains Public Library

3 3455 01773 7450

D0461675

Presented to the

Northern Plains
Public Library

In memory of
Elizabeth A. Eisenhauer

Never Cry Werewolf

HEATHER DAVIS

Never Cry Werewolf

Northern Plains Public Library
Ault Colorado

An Imprint of HarperCollins*Publishers*

HarperTeen is an imprint of HarperCollins Publishers.

Never Cry Werewolf
Copyright © 2009 by Heather Davis
All rights reserved. Printed in the United States of America.
No part of this book may be used or reproduced in any
manner whatsoever without written permission except in
the case of brief quotations embodied in critical articles
and reviews. For information address HarperCollins
Children's Books, a division of HarperCollins Publishers,
10 East 53rd Street, New York, NY 10022.
www.harperteen.com

Library of Congress Cataloging-in-Publication Data
Davis, Heather, date
    Never cry werewolf / Heather Davis. — 1st ed.
        p.   cm.
    Summary: Forced to attend a camp for teens with
behavior problems, sixteen-year-old Shelby Locke's
attempts to follow the rules go astray when she meets a
handsome, British werewolf.
    ISBN 978-0-06-134923-2
    [1. Werewolves—Fiction. 2. Camps—Fiction.
3. Interpersonal relations—Fiction. 4. Behavior—
Fiction.] I. Title.
PZ7.D28845Ne 2009   2008051967
[Fic]—dc22   CIP
                                                         AC

Typography by Andrea Vandergrift

09 10 11 12 13   LP/RRDB   10 9 8 7 6 5 4 3 2 1
❖
First Edition

☾

*For my father, John-Carl, who taught me to believe,
and for my mother, Jude, who taught me to howl*

ONE

Moonlight has special powers. Even in Beverly Hills, where everything sparkles whether it's real or fake, there's something magic about that big full moon. It can make you act crazy, take a risk you'd never consider in the daylight, or even fall completely head over heels. Moonlight can totally change your life. And it all starts so simply.

You. Him. The moon. You're toast.

Take a moonlit night last April, for example. The garden practically glowed with moon magic. I felt it all around me, closing in.

The boy of the moment was Josh Tilton, the senior from my fourth-period art class, looking oh-so-delicious in Levi's and a gray T. Fully under the moon's spell himself, Josh paused by one of our prize rosebushes and plucked a perfect white bud. "For you, Shelby," he said, his voice barely above a whisper.

It was way more romantic than him sharing his popcorn

with me at the Cineplex earlier that night. In fact, it was, like, the most perfect moment ever, so I didn't tell him my stepmother was going to freak when she noticed the bloom clipped. Instead, I sniffed the rose while I watched Josh's blue eyes shimmering in the moonlight. The swoony feeling in my stomach intensified. Pure magic.

"So," he whispered, "do you want to go to the prom?"

Um, you're super cute— Duh! I sucked in a breath and said, "That would be so—"

Suddenly, the sprinklers whooshed on.

"Crap!" I shrieked. Like a dork, I stood there blindly trying to bat away the water until Josh pulled me and my face out of the *tick-tick-tick* of the spray, and we took cover under the orange tree that separated the garden from the lawn.

Cold water from my hair dripped down my back, but I was so embarrassed by my sprinkler dance, I pretended not to mind. "Well, that was refreshing," I said with a forced giggle. My heart hammered in my chest, but I didn't know if it was from the humiliation or from the nearness of Josh.

"Your gardener has perfect timing," he said, brushing his thumb against my cheek, wiping away water. Little drops sparkled on his eyelashes as he gazed down at my lips. Oh, man. He wanted to kiss me. "So, do you wanna?"

I knew he was talking about the prom, but I was focused on his lips. "Duh. I mean, yeah," I mumbled.

And then he did it. He leaned in for a kiss. A kiss I'd been praying for ever since the first day of spring. A kiss I knew was going to be the most romantic ever . . .

"Can't you take a *hint*?" My stepmother's voice sawed through the magical moonlight. "Or do I need to get the *hose*?"

Lights blazed to life all around us, causing Josh to jump back a good foot. And my stepmother, Priscilla, who my dad called Honey Bun, marched toward us across the soaking lawn. She didn't seem to care that the water would wreck her suede stilettos.

"Step away from the boy!" she said.

"You've got to be kidding," I fired back. "I'm helping Josh with his posters for the charity car wash."

"In the dark?" Priscilla's frown deepened.

"Well, we're not making the posters *now*, obviously," I said.

Josh stepped toward her. "Let me explain," he began.

Priscilla smiled thinly at Josh. "That's not necessary. I see exactly what's going on here. Romeo, you can hit the road. And Shelby, you're coming with me."

In sixty seconds flat, Priscilla had me up to the house and sweating under a crystal chandelier that now reminded me of a naked lightbulb in a police station. In the too-tight black dress she'd worn out to dinner with my dad, Priscilla circled the dining room table like a seasoned interrogator. "Your father will be very disappointed," she began. "This is a clear violation of the house rules."

I raised my head, listening. Yep. Dad's uneven snores floated down from the master suite upstairs. My guess was that Priscilla had volunteered for guard duty. After all, she'd had her eye on me since the moment she married Dad last year. And the more she watched, the more I tried to give her something *to* watch.

"This is the final straw," she said, pointing at me with one of her daggerlike red fingernails. "Your father distinctly told you no dating. Period. A justifiable rule after the latest *incident* with that Sawyer boy."

Yes. The latest incident. Wes Sawyer. She didn't need to remind me. Dad's two-hour lecture on trusting the wrong people had been enough. And, seriously, how was I to know the Porsche belonged to Wes's vacationing neighbor? Wes had picked me up to help him study for his biology final because he was on the verge of failing the class. But apparently that didn't count for anything after our stop to get snacks at the In-N-Out Burger stand. The cops hadn't liked the steamed-up windows of the Porsche. Neither had Dad.

I leaned back in the dining room chair and gave Priscilla my best bring-it-on look. "Yeah. Thanks for that. Wes *loves* that military academy. Apparently, he's up for honor cadet this month."

Priscilla's heavily made-up eyes narrowed. "Very funny, but I doubt you'll ever go joyriding again."

"It's too early to tell." I gave her my best evil eye—but she, being a complete pro, returned one twice as ugly. The evil-eye contest only ended when we both noticed my father, in his bathrobe and slippers, yawning in the doorway.

"What's going on?" he asked. "Shelby, are you just getting in? What time is it?"

"It's twelve thirty," Priscilla answered quickly.

"You're an hour late?" Dad scratched at his hair, which stuck up at all angles like a crazy scientist's hair should. Typically, Dad never remembered the ordinary things—like brushing his hair, buying milk, gassing up the car, or feeding goldfish. But, since his big chemical discovery, we could pay people to do those chores on a daily basis. Well, except for the hair brushing.

"Hey, Dad," I said, mentally preparing my defense. "Technically, I've been home for an hour. I was out in the garden, but I *was* home."

Priscilla shook her head. "With a boy."

"You see, Dad—"

"In the moonlight," she added, throwing him a knowing look.

Dad sighed loud and long. "Shelby, we've had this talk."

I held up a hand. "Before you go there, he's nothing like Wes. Josh is responsible, I swear. And he really needed my help tonight."

"Shelby, you don't have to save the world at the expense of yourself," said Dad. "Your heart is in the right place, but sometimes your first impressions about these boys aren't reliable." He pulled a chair out from the dining room table and sat down across from me.

"What are you talking about? I have excellent people instincts." I gestured toward Priscilla with my head to say hello-didn't-I-warn-you-about-her, but Dad ignored me.

"You can't keep jumping in with both feet and forget to

consider the consequences. You have to be responsible." He was giving me his scientist face. The one that always makes me feel like some kind of lab rat. "You were supposed to be working on weighing the pros and cons of your choices."

"I did, Dad. Josh needed some help making the posters for the charity car wash next weekend. We're going to raise money for an animal shelter."

Dad furrowed his brows at me. "And did you make the posters?"

"Earlier, yeah. I didn't think it was a big deal."

"So this wasn't like the time you helped that boy Sam with his Mark Twain paper?"

I shook my head. "Dad, seriously. Not Mark Twain. Jane Austen."

Dad sighed. "What I mean is, you weren't at Josh's house unsupervised? His parents were home?"

"Uh . . . well—"

Priscilla shook her head. "Let's get to the real issue. You lied, Shelby. You told us you were making posters with your friends and then you were going to the movies with Lauren."

"She was *there*. It was a group of us, Dad. And besides, I didn't even get to tell you the best part—Josh wants me to go to the prom with him. Josh Tilton! He's like the smartest boy in school. Going to Harvard or something, I swear."

"Shelby," Dad said, punctuating it with a long sigh and a glance toward Honey Bun. "You're not going to the prom. I'm afraid I can't allow it. Not after tonight's shenanigans."

"Shenanigans? Making posters for homeless dogs is not shenanigans."

Dad gave me a doubtful look.

"It's not like the other times, okay? Please don't take the prom away from me. I found this great dress at Fred Segal. It'd be so perfect." I pictured me in the dress. Petal pink and floor length, it totally camouflaged my storklike legs and made my chest seem fuller, which was huge for me. When you're built like a stick figure, a dress that good isn't easy to find.

"Shelby, you're only a sophomore. There will be other proms." Priscilla shrugged. "And while we're on the subject of clothing, that *outfit* isn't appropriate at your age."

My mouth dropped open. I was wearing a cami with a lace shrug and a mini. It was so not slutty compared to Priscilla's wardrobe. I mean, if I'd wanted to go all hoochie, I would have borrowed her low-cut wrap dress like I did the time I sneaked into that club on Sunset.

As it was, I dressed like my friends at school. We weren't super smart or anything. We definitely weren't drama or band kids. Some of us played on the soccer team, but mostly we shopped and we dated. Well, mostly my friends shopped and I dated. We were on the edge of popularity, the edge that money always provides. On that particular edge you have to be fashion conscious, but I wasn't going to turn into a Beverly Hills stereotype. The fact that I was still a brunette totally proved that. But I guess Priscilla thought I should dress like a nun or something.

Priscilla hopped all over my stunned silence. "You ought to be presenting yourself as a lady and—"

"Why don't you sit down, Honey Bun," Dad said, finally shutting Priscilla up.

She reluctantly sank into one of the fancy upholstered chairs.

"Shelby," Dad said, "we trusted you to be where you said you were going to be, and with who you said you were going to be with. Trust is a fragile thing."

"May I say something?" Priscilla gritted her bleached teeth, which against the bloodred color of her lipstick made her look like a vampire ready to feed. "This whole situation is very disappointing. I can't believe you're manipulating your father like this, Shelby."

Manipulating? That was interesting coming from her. Priscilla was the one who'd thrown herself at Dad at the plastic surgeons' convention where he was unveiling his miracle drug and then manipulated our whole lives.

My dad's really a simple guy, so maybe he was too dazzled by Priscilla's boob job and her flashy clothes to see what she really was. Since my mom had died three years ago, Dad had been seriously lacking in the dating department. He was ripe for the gold digging and Priscilla knew it.

Less than four months after they had met, just as stock in Dad's company split, making him the first multimillionaire in our Milwaukee neighborhood, Priscilla had convinced him to marry her in a tacky, huge wedding fit for the E! channel. But her best work was talking Dad into moving us away from my life and friends to this fortress in Beverly Hills. When I asked why we had to leave, Dad told me it was because we needed a fresh start. But I always thought it was because Priscilla would be closer to her plastic surgeon.

"It's late," Dad said, scratching at his crazy hair again. "You should get to bed, Shelby. We all should."

I shrugged.

"Yes. Let's continue this discussion in the morning. Remember, dear, we have some *options*," Priscilla said, giving Dad a knowing glance. Before I could ask what that was all about, she whisked him up the staircase to bed.

I was left wondering what she meant by *options*. Unfortunately, it wouldn't be long before I found out.

I slept terribly that night. Peeking through my window, the face of the full moon kept me awake like a giant lighted clock dial. Over and over, I thought about what Priscilla must be planning. I mean, they'd already taken the prom away. What else could they do?

It wasn't like I was a bad kid. Sure, I stayed out late sometimes, but that was only because I couldn't stand being around Priscilla, especially when she was draping herself all over Dad. And they didn't need to keep harping at me about hanging out with boys. I got good grades, so it wasn't my fault that guys from school wanted help and that sometimes meant

I got distracted and lost track of time. I didn't think there was anything wrong with helping someone out, especially a cute guy.

For the record, I was trying to be more responsible lately. I now knew that sneaking out of the house to help with a last-minute history project could turn into joyriding. I'd figured out that tutoring a running back from the football team sometimes led to getting caught making out in the reference section of the library. I totally got it. And now that I was trying to follow the rules, a simple walk in the moonlight had ruined everything.

And what about Josh Tilton? I doubted he was in any kind of trouble. I was the one taking the fall for a boy who dared to push the rules and make me break my curfew. Life was so unfair.

Priscilla and Dad were on the stone patio eating breakfast when I finally went downstairs the next morning. Against the velvet green of the lawn behind them, they looked like a picture-perfect couple, right down to their fancy tennis clothes. I hadn't even brushed my hair.

I padded up to the table and plunked down into one of the white iron chairs.

"There's my sleepyhead," Dad said.

I gave him a half smile. He hadn't called me "sleepyhead" in a long time.

"Here you go," he said, handing me a glass of the fresh-squeezed orange juice he'd poured from the crystal pitcher on the table.

Priscilla lowered her fashion magazine and gave me a perfunctory smile. "Good morning, Shelby."

"Hi." I took a swig of the juice and reached for a piece of toast.

Dad passed the strawberry jam without me even asking. I slathered my toast with it, and then paused. It was too quiet. And everyone was being too nice. It was weird.

"Okay. What's going on?" I said, setting down my toast and knife.

Dad cleared his throat. "Honey Bun and I feel like you need a break."

"Summer's almost here, Dad. I'll get a two-month break."

"No," Priscilla said, tucking a strand of her black hair behind an ear. "What your father means is a break from us."

"I will be having a break. My friends and I were talking about a trip to Cabo."

"No." Priscilla placed a hand on one of my father's. "I'm afraid not. Mike?"

"Ah . . . we've been talking it over," Dad said, "and we feel that perhaps some time away with counseling and fresh air would be ideal."

My heart started to pound. "Counseling?"

Dad nodded. "Some time to spend working on yourself."

"Yes," said Priscilla in a silky tone. "At a top-notch teen program at an exclusive facility."

Oh, crap. She meant brat camp. I remembered the stories from school about the kids who were sent away to hike in the

11

mountains for the summer at one of those "top-notch" programs. They came back all brainwashed, like totally different people. I'm sure that was just what Priscilla was hoping.

While I stewed, Priscilla calmly reached into her Coach tote and pulled out a stack of slick brochures. She fanned them out on the table in front of my father and me. "My favorite of these is Red Canyon Ranch, a personal skill-building institute in the Utah desert."

"Wait. Dad, *you* actually think I should go to a brat camp?" I couldn't keep the anger from my voice. No one had ever called me a brat. Certainly not my dad, who, up until Priscilla had hypnotized him, had been semi-reasonable.

"I need to be able to trust you again. Some time apart might be good." Dad looked down at the table, like he was embarrassed to regurgitate Priscilla's fake reason. "A camp like this might help teach you some life skills, give you some perspective."

"Thanks. It really feels good to have your own dad throw you to the wolves," I said, in total disbelief that he was selling me out.

Dad held my gaze for a moment, looking like he wanted to say something. I hoped he was going to tell me this was all a bad idea and just to forget it. But he didn't. He gazed at me in a sad, tired way—a way that seemed to say he didn't know what to do with me. It hurt to see that in his eyes.

I picked up one of the brochures, just so I didn't have to face him.

"Maybe it could be fun," he said.

Eww. The kids on the Camp Sweetwater brochure made me cringe. They looked like they were being held at gunpoint and forced to smile.

But Dad didn't seem bothered. "'Nestled in the majestic mountains of western Montana, Camp Sweetwater is the most effective remote teen therapy facility in the nation.' You love the mountains. It'd be beautiful up there," he said, with what I hoped was fake enthusiasm.

I paged through a few more brochures, and then finally I held up the Red Canyon brochure. "Priscilla's favorite says 'boot camp' workouts. Five-mile runs in the *desert*? That sounds like hell on earth."

"Shelby, language," whispered Priscilla. "And desert air can be really good for your skin. People pay thousands for workouts at desert spas."

"It's not a spa, that's the problem." I glared at her and then turned to Dad. "You want me to run in the desert? Am I that bad of a kid?"

He didn't answer, just continued paging through another brochure. "Swimming, arts and crafts, archery," he said with a hopeful smile. "They sound like normal camps."

"Normal camps do not serve therapy with their s'mores," I said.

Dad regained his serious face. "Here, listen to this one: 'Campers learn self-respect and discipline along with the joy of helping others. After experiencing community service projects, our graduates go on to lead productive lives filled with solid American values.'"

"Discipline? Community service projects?" I shuddered, imagining myself in a baggy orange jumpsuit picking up trash along the side of the road. "Summer is supposed to be fun."

Dad patted my hand. "Keep looking. There's bound to be one you'd like."

"I've already made a call to Red Canyon," Priscilla said in a breezy tone. "They have a place for you if you'd like to give it a try. A little discipline and physical conditioning would be good for you."

"I want you to have a say in this, Shelby. Pick the one that you think you'd enjoy," Dad said, giving Priscilla a back-off look.

Reluctantly, I started reading the brochures seriously. Camp after camp promising to return well-adjusted teens at the end of summer. Lists of disorders and problems they could treat. Glossy photographs of immaculate campuses and barracklike rooms. My stomach felt sicker as the minutes went by.

Finally, after discarding a few more with pictures of kids smiling like zombies, I picked up a brochure with mountains on the front.

Deep in the Oregon forests, Camp Crescent is an exclusive facility tailored to the individual. We strive not to change young people into someone their parents think they should be, but to deepen their understanding of who they are. Transformations happen every summer at Camp Crescent through traditional camp activities and a variety of artistic expression exercises.

I let out a deep breath. "At least this one doesn't sound like torture or brainwashing."

"Camp Crescent is a good start," Priscilla said with a shrug. "But it may not have the discipline you need. I'm going to have Red Canyon save you a place."

"How about neither one?" I said, beginning a last desperate attempt. "I know I haven't exactly been the perfect daughter lately, but—"

Priscilla faked a cough and slanted her eyes toward Dad.

I tried to ignore her, realizing I was fighting for more than my summer. "Listen, I'll try to follow all your rules. I'll try to be nice to Honey Bun. Please, don't make me go." But even as I said the words, I knew it was too late.

Priscilla's smile told me I was already gone.

TWO

The last weeks of school went by, the senior prom came and went—Josh Tilton took Sophie Brewer, Honor Society vice president—and my carefree life spiraled downward. The moon magic had totally worn off.

So, the second week of June, I found myself in a mess of kids gathering around the Camp Crescent bus in a parking lot at the Portland airport. As I dug in my backpack for a stick of gum, a girl in sunglasses tugged on my sleeve. She reminded me of an elf. Not the tall *Lord of the Rings* kind, the toy-building North Pole kind.

Her tiny face paled against her blue-black hair as she asked, "Weren't you on my flight from LAX?"

I nodded. I'd noticed her reading a copy of *Paris Match* a few rows away from me on the plane. "Yeah, that was me," I said.

She nodded back, then stared at the sprinkle of afternoon

rain sizzling on the warm pavement, apparently ignoring me now that she knew where I was from. So much for elfin conversation.

To pass the time, I put on lip gloss and fluffed my hair, using my mirror to check out the guys behind us in line. Some of them had potential, especially a tall blond guy who resembled Brad Pitt when I squinted really hard. But, I reminded myself, the last thing I needed to be focused on was boys. I had to make it through the summer and stay far away from anything resembling desert sand and military uniforms.

The line inched forward, placing me in front of the luggage compartment, which overflowed with matching Louis Vuitton travel sets and expensive hiking gear. I handed my plain red American Tourister to the pimply guy loading the bags.

"Sheep," said Elf Girl, dragging an airport cart of luggage toward the guy.

"Excuse me?"

"They buy the designer labels like sheep." She shrugged. "Like it really matters what your camping stuff is packed in."

"Easy for you to say," said a redheaded girl, cutting in line in front of us. "When you're a billionaire, I guess first impressions don't matter." She shoved a huge monogrammed suitcase toward the bag dude, then studied my blank face. "She's Ariel DeVoisier? The perfume heiress?"

"Oh." I blinked at her. "Great." DeVoisier? I'd seen the name at the makeup counter, but Elf Girl sure didn't seem all glamorous or anything. Her black cardigan was buttoned all the way to the top, and her tan capris were pretty normal. Her sunglasses did have little rhinestones in the corners, though.

Meanwhile, the redhead smiled. "I'm Jenna Grant. My dad's in real estate in South Beach." She did a sort of twirl, showing off her hot-pink jacket and her matching mini. "Prada."

"Nice," I said with a shrug. It was a cute outfit and all, but not the best for camping, obviously. Besides, I wasn't too impressed by the whole Prada thing. I mean, seriously, a year ago when I lived in Milwaukee, my friends all shopped at Old Navy. Nobody cared about what you wore, just if you looked good in it.

Jenna looked me up and down, as if trying to use X-ray vision to check out my labels. "I'm sorry—and you are?"

From her snotty tone, I guessed she wasn't satisfied with my lackluster reaction or with my outfit of American Eagle shorts, Roxy zip sweatshirt, and tank. Labels aside, I'm no fashionista or anything. Some makeup essentials, a few highlights to brighten up my boring brown hair, and I'm good to go. I gave her a confident smile and said, "I'm Shelby Locke."

"Wait—of *Locke* Cosmeceuticals?" replied Jenna in a breathless voice.

"Yeah. So?"

"No waaaay!" Jenna's eyes widened. "My mother *swears* by Re-Gen. Those Botox people are losing a fortune on her. Re-Gen, unbelievable."

All of a sudden, the entire line of kids clustered around me, talking about Re-Gen. Ariel hung back, seeming to be the only one not interested in Dad's plastic surgery drug. Meanwhile, everyone was chattering about their parents' plastic surgeons or someone they knew who wanted Re-Gen. It was creepy. At least at my school, everyone was over everyone else's fame or money or whatever.

My cheeks flaming hot, I backed away from the crowd. "It's no big deal," I said.

"Boys and girls, we need to maintain an orderly check-in." An old guy with a mustache and a beer belly barely hidden by a Camp Crescent polo shirt clapped his hands near the bus doors. "In line, now!"

Grumbling, everyone fell back into place.

"So, you're, like, a celebrity," mumbled Ariel. "Yay for you."

"Yeah," I said, arching an eyebrow at her. "Yay for me, Miss Billionaire."

Ariel hid behind her fringe of straight black bangs, but I did see her smile.

After hearing about Re-Gen, Jenna apparently decided I was somebody she should get to know. She blabbed away about her family's second home in the Hamptons, and her mother's private raw food chef, who made the most divine organic fennel carpaccio, whatever that was. By the time we'd reached the front of the line, my brain hurt.

"Howdy, I'm Mr. Winters," the old guy said, checking my name off on his clipboard. "Deposit your cell phones, PDAs, MP3 players, and any other electronics into the bin on the front seat."

19

"My PDA?" I clutched my backpack to my chest. I'd wanted to text my friends a daily camp report.

"You'll barely miss it," said Mr. Winters with a thin smile.

Ariel rolled her eyes but dug out her cell phone.

Mr. Winters tapped his pen against his clipboard. "Let's go, girls, we're on a schedule."

And with that, I climbed into the darkened bus and chucked my last link to the outside world into a plastic bin.

Reading steadily as the bus rolled away the miles, I was halfway through a romance paperback when we jerked to a stop. I looked out the window and saw that a black limo had pulled up next to us on the shoulder of the road.

"Sit tight, campers. This will only take a second," said Mr. Winters, bounding to the front of the bus.

Jenna, who'd taken the seat across from me and Ariel, said, "Why couldn't *I* ride in a limo from the airport?"

The boys behind us hooted and laughed. One of the guys leaned forward. It was the blond guy from the line—my squinty-eyed Brad Pitt. "There's always one at every camp."

I raised my eyebrows. "One what?"

"A prima donna," he said with a twist of his lips that was almost a sneer.

"Oh-kaay." I gave him a nod and settled back into my seat.

"Watch out for that guy," Ariel whispered to me. "Charles Morton. Totally nuts. His dad owns seven tabloid newspapers

20

worldwide. A few years ago, he tried to buy his way out of Pinnacle Crest Camp in Idaho by promising to get the counselor Reese Witherspoon's cell number. When that didn't work he tried to run away. They found him hitchhiking along the interstate. He's totally whacked."

"Sounds like it." I gave Ariel a little smile, impressed by how dialed in she was. "The brat camp world must be very small."

She nodded. "I see some of the same kids at camp every year. Everyone's parents keep shelling out money when these stupid places don't work. They'll probably keep sending us here until we go off to college."

I wondered why Ariel kept getting sent to camp, but I didn't ask her. It was probably something like my situation—evil stepmother trying to ruin her life, or her parents too distracted to care.

"So, have you been to Camp Crescent before?" I asked.

"No, but it's cushy compared to the place I was last year." Ariel's elfin smile dimmed.

"What camp are you talking about? Was it really that bad?"

"Red Canyon Ranch. Every time I say its name the scar from my scorpion sting flares up."

I blinked at her. "Hot desert boot camp? Third level of hell, right?" I said, thinking she was joking, but Ariel didn't laugh.

"It almost killed me last summer," she said with a shudder.

I peered into her eyes to see if she was serious, and what I

21

saw there gave me a chill. "Uh . . . my stepmother said if things don't work out here, I'd end up there," I said.

Ariel's mouth tightened. "Trust me. It's horrible. People are always yelling at you, barking orders, making you run miles in the sand dunes."

"So the brochure doesn't lie," I said.

"Actually, it leaves a lot of things out," Ariel said. "They have this solitary confinement place called the Thinking Shack. I got sent there once for twenty-four hours because I made my bed the wrong way by accident."

"No way."

"That wasn't the worst, though, Shelby. They try to tear you down and make you into some kind of robot."

Just then the bus shook with the clamping noise of the luggage compartment shutting. As the limo sped away, Mr. Winters lumbered back up the steps, along with a boy— not the type of guy you'd think was cute right away but definitely the type that made you want to keep looking.

Dark hair spilled down his forehead, and his olive-toned skin gleamed in the dim light. He was tall, with long arms. A leather jacket, a black concert T-shirt, worn Levi's, and motorcycle boots showed he was anything but a preppy jock like some of the boys on the bus. And he hadn't gone the all-black route like some of the Goth guys. He stood in the aisle motionless, like he was daring anyone to say something.

Ah, yes. The rebel troublemaker common to every school I'd ever heard of, let alone attended. The cute bad boy you date and he wrecks your life. I wasn't impressed. But when he took off his sunglasses, I found myself staring into deep, amber brown eyes.

"Austin Bridges the Third," whispered Ariel, giving him a little wave. "What is he doing here?"

"What? He's not a brat camp regular?" I said.

Ariel shook her head. "Never."

Jenna leaned across the aisle. "Do you know him?" she gushed.

Ariel nodded. "His dad and his entourage stay at our beach house when they tour So Cal. We know them, all right."

"Oh, wait. Bridges? That's the son of that crazy lead singer from Burning Bridges?" I said, wrinkling up my nose.

Ariel and Jenna looked at me like I was crazy.

"Sorry. I have heard of them, but I don't keep up with dried-up old rock stars," I said with a little shrug.

"Austin was on the cover of *People* three months ago with his dad," said Jenna.

"I must have missed it," I murmured.

The guys behind us let out a little whoop as Austin searched for a seat. "'Dancing on your grave! I'll be dancing on your grave, dearie!'" they sang, butchering lyrics from Burning Bridges's last hit.

Austin glared over at them, shutting them right up. "Have we a problem, lads?"

Ooh. British accent alert. I loved accents. I sat up straighter to make sure I didn't miss a word.

As the bus lurched forward, Austin slid his backpack off his shoulder and took an empty seat a few rows in front of us, his eyes still on the doofs behind us. The glare was so hot now, I swear I almost saw smoke rising up.

"Well? Have we?" Austin said.

Charles turned red. "Chill, man. We were just singing."

"As you Yanks are fond of saying, don't quit your day job," Austin said tartly.

Hmm . . . I stopped watching, and went back to reading my paperback romance. Well, pretending to read, anyway. My eyes were on the glossy hair of Austin Bridges III.

Camp just got a whole lot more interesting.

After what seemed like an eternity, the paved road ended, and the bus shot into a tunnel of dense evergreen trees. From the bus window, it was trunk after trunk as far back as you could see. Tangles of berry brambles, prehistoric-looking giant ferns, and scrubby underbrush filled out what few holes there were in the forest landscape. Saturated green and brown everywhere, it was the biggest dose of nature I'd seen since we'd moved to California.

"A forbidden forest," said Ariel.

I studied her serious expression and then said, "Okay, I just have to know—do you speak Elvish?"

Ariel narrowed her eyes at me. "What?"

"Nothing. It's just, I mean, 'a forbidden forest'?"

"You know," Ariel said. "Like in a fairy tale. It's dark and

24

dangerous. The kind of place you go into and never return from. Or you go in there and the trees talk and there are magic creatures."

"Uh-huh . . ."

"Now you think I'm weird," Ariel said.

"No, no. I think you have a great imagination," I said. "But I'm pretty sure it's just regular old woods."

Ariel looked indignant. "Actually, I heard a kid ran off and died out there in the forest a few years ago."

"They probably tell campers that to keep them from running away."

Ariel shrugged. "There are cougars all over the Pacific Northwest. Not to mention coyotes, black bears, even a grizzly once in a while. I wouldn't want to take my chances."

I glanced again at Ariel's prim yet funky outfit—very Manhattan. I didn't guess she got to go on nature hikes very often. In fact, most of these kids didn't seem the camping type. But when you're going somewhere for therapy, maybe the camping is secondary.

"See how the trees stretch into the horizon," Ariel said in a quiet voice. "It's like another world."

"Yeah, maybe—"

Suddenly, the bus swerved violently. Several girls, and a few boys, screamed. Mr. Winters, who I could barely hear above the kids heckling the screaming boys, came on over the loudspeaker. "Folks, the bus has a flat tire. There's no reason for alarm. Return to your seats. Stay calm."

"Stay calm," muttered Ariel as the bus limped off the road. "They always say that at brat camp, but no one ever does."

An hour later, we were still stuck in our seats, waiting for some mythical replacement bus. The mood was barely above riot stage as a tall lady counselor with a flowery dress and a guitar strummed out the last awful chorus of a song about fried ham.

Mr. Winters, who'd been handling complaints for fifty-nine of the last sixty minutes, reached for the intercom. "Okay, campers. We'll get off the bus to stretch our legs while we wait," he announced. "Just five minutes, folks. And stay close. We don't want to lose anyone."

Outside, people plopped their backpacks down on the grassy shoulder of the road. Of course, some boys, and even a few girls, headed for the woods to pee, with Guitar Lady and Mr. Winters watching from the tree line. It seemed pretty permissive of Mr. Winters. I mean, any second a kid could—

"Hey!" A shout rattled the windows of the bus and bounced off the endless tree trunks. "Mr. Winters!" A nerdy boy dressed in baggy khakis and an oversize pink polo bounded out of the trees. "Some kid took off running into the woods!"

Winters nearly dropped the megaphone. "What? Where?"

The snitch dragged the old man into the woods, pointing into the distance. A lot of kids ran over from their spots near the bus, despite Winters yelling into the bullhorn to stay back. Guitar Lady snatched up her instrument, trying to distract everyone with another chorus of "Fried Ham." That totally bombed. Kids lined the edge of the woods, trying to see what was happening.

Ariel and I followed Jenna over to the tree line, avoiding the clumps of backpacks and lounging slackers who were too lazy to come gawk at the disturbance.

As we reached the end of the grassy meadow, Austin stepped out from behind a tree.

"Hello again," he said to Ariel. Then his gaze moved to me.

"Hey, Austin. Oh, this is Shelby Locke," Ariel said. "Shelby, Austin Bridges."

He gave me a little nod.

"What are you doing here?" Ariel asked.

Austin's gaze darkened. "It's a bloody mistake. My father's new road manager is a complete idjit," he said. "So, what's all the ruckus? Someone stray from the pack?"

"He was probably trying to get away from the awful songs," I said.

"What's up?" Vince, the preppy black kid who'd been sitting behind me on the bus, joined the group of us standing opposite Austin. Vince was the son of some film director guy I'd barely heard of.

"Just wondering who's playing hide-and-seek with Mr. Winters," Jenna said in a bored tone.

"Wait." Vince turned and scanned the crowd near the bus, concern in his dark brown eyes. "Where's Charles? You know, that skinny kid who was sitting next to me?" He ran a hand over the back of his shaved neck. "I could be wrong, but I don't see him."

27

"Everyone step away from the woods," shouted Guitar Lady. "Grab your gear and we'll reboard the bus."

We started to do that, but then we heard Winters wailing, "Cha-arles!" into the megaphone and we all stopped.

Vince shook his head. "Great," he said. "I didn't want to be right."

"He's probably just pulling a prank," said Jenna.

"I don't know. Maybe. A minute ago he was over there by our backpacks," Vince replied. "I thought he was just getting a snack or something, but I guess he bailed."

Austin's gaze snapped to the pile of gear. "That wanker's really gone." His mouth set in a thin line, Austin walked toward our stuff.

We all followed, but as everyone grabbed their gear, Austin didn't have a backpack. That was weird because I swear I saw everyone put their stuff all in one pile.

"Everything all right?" I asked.

Austin raised his gaze to me, and for half a second I thought I saw something flicker in his eyes, some unreadable expression. "Must be here somewhere," he mumbled.

Just then a crashing sound echoed through the woods. Flailing his limbs, the snitch stumbled back through the trees, then fell in a heap at our feet. "He's gone," he said, panting. "Mr. Winters said . . . to come back . . . to keep . . . myself from getting lost."

"Thank goodness," said Jenna dryly. "We wouldn't want anything to happen to you."

Austin paced alongside the group, visibly upset. I hadn't taken him for the type who'd worry about another kid, especially one who'd made fun of him on the bus, so I was a little surprised.

Somewhere off in the distance, the droning pattern of Winters's megaphone started up again. "Cha-arles! Cha-arles!" It was a lonesome sound that made the air seem heavier, the shady meadow a little darker. Beyond the clearing, the forest loomed vast and ominous, the dense trees a canopy that blocked out all the sunlight.

I shuddered.

"I told you guys, it's probably just a prank. That guy probably has a martyr complex or he's just trying to get attention. It's so juvenile," said Jenna, shaking her head.

"Cha-arles! Cha-arles!"

We all looked at each other. No one was smiling. I thought of Ariel's forbidden forest stuff and almost felt sorry for Charles.

Austin, meanwhile, had turned toward the woods, his dark hair rustling in the slight breeze. "My bag," he muttered.

"What?" I asked.

He took a step toward the forest, and I reached for his arm.

"Whatever it is, just stay here, okay?" I said.

"Shelby," he said, shrugging away from me, "don't say a word."

And before I could stop him, he raced into the trees.

29

THREE

"C ome back!" Guitar Lady shrieked, running after Austin. "You come back here this instant!"

Gazing into the endless green and brown landscape, I couldn't even pick Austin out anymore. The forest seemed to swallow him up.

"Dude moves quick," said Vince with appreciation.

After banging her guitar on, like, forty trees, Guitar Lady returned, scowling. "No one else leaves!" she barked, the happy counselor routine totally over.

"What's up with Austin?" Ariel said in a low whisper.

"I think Charles took his backpack. Austin's just after his stuff," I said, shrugging. It wasn't like Austin was risking his hide to go save someone. Guys like him didn't do that kind of thing. Not even the British ones.

Minutes dragged by as we hung out on the grass near the bus, talking in between listening for news. Some of the kids were bored or annoyed, because they apparently couldn't wait to get to camp. I started to worry about Austin and Charles, and even the old guy. I hoped Ariel's wild animal stories were made up.

"I've searched all along the road," Mr. Winters's voice hissed over Guitar Lady's walkie-talkie. "Any sign of the replacement bus? Over."

"Not yet. Over."

"Heading toward the river. I think he might—" Mr. Winters's voice faded out into a crackle of static.

"Mr. Winters? Come in. Hello? Over?" Guitar Lady said in a shrill tone.

I shivered. Mr. Winters must have been deep in the woods now, out of range.

Feigning calmness, Guitar Lady slipped her radio back into her pocket and reached for her guitar. "Alrighty. Let's have a song."

I groaned and opened my paperback. Ariel let out a deep sigh and stared into the woods, legends of the lost camper probably tumbling through her mind.

Meanwhile, Vince was starting to freak. "What idiots! Charles is from Palo Alto, what does he know about the woods? I mean, camp sucks, but it's not worth risking your life. And what's up with the British dude? They're gonna get eaten by a bear or something."

"It could totally happen. There are all kinds of animals out there," Ariel said.

"Maybe," I murmured, setting down my book. "But they could also get hurt or get lost or suffer exposure to the elements if the temperature dips. Do you think they have any survival skills?"

Vince stuffed his hands into the pockets of his baggy jeans. "Like what?"

"Like starting a fire? Or building a shelter?" I asked.

"We did that at Outdoor Adventure Team two summers ago, with the counselors," offered Ariel.

"I was there once," Jenna said, turning to me. "Trust me—it's no adventure. They teach you how to climb smelly ropes and make you eat dehydrated lentil stew."

That didn't sound like camping to me. Back before Priscilla, my family used to go camping a lot. It was way more involved than climbing ropes, especially in the dense woods of northern Wisconsin. And when your dad is a former Eagle Scout, every-thing gets done by the book whether you like it or not. "I never had to eat dehydrated lentils," I said.

"Lucky you," said Jenna with a shudder. "Freshly cooked lentils are so much better."

"Children, I can't hear you singing," called Guitar Lady, glancing over at our group.

"*Children?* Really," I muttered.

Time crawled by as everybody sat mumbling the words to another inane song. My gaze never left the trees. A cool breeze tickled the back of my neck and I pulled my sweatshirt's hood up. The dense forest was definitely not as warm as California, and the nights would be even colder. It wasn't bad for me—I'd

camped in way worse conditions up in northern Wisconsin—
but a Brit, an out-of-shape old guy, and a wuss really would be
bear bait.

"Children!" Out of breath, Guitar Lady clapped her hands
and pointed. A bus rolled down the dirt road toward us. Some
of the kids cheered.

Not me. I'd been looking forward to the dumb bus's arrival,
but for some reason, since Austin disappeared, I didn't want to
go anywhere. I placed a hand over my queasy stomach. All I
had to do was get to camp. Do my time. Stick to the rules. Stay
far, far away from that Red Canyon place. So why did I feel like
I should be doing something to help?

Clapping her hands again, Guitar Lady summoned us over
as the new bus rattled to a halt. "Grab your bags, campers."

"What about those kids in the forest?" I said. "We can't
leave them."

Guitar Lady smiled with practiced patience. "Mr. Winters
will find the boys and telephone us at the camp. We'll send the
bus back for them."

"How do you know he'll find them?" I demanded. "There
should be a search-and-rescue team here. An ambulance or
something. I mean, aren't you worried? That's dense forest
out there."

Guitar Lady's smile disappeared. "That's for the adults to
worry about," she said. "Your job is to worry about *you*. And
right now, *you* need to get on the bus." Her beady eyes burned
down on me with precision.

This lady, with her totally power-hungry attitude, was starting to remind me of Priscilla. I had the sudden urge to smash her guitar so she'd never be able to torture us again with songs about lunch meat, but that'd probably be a bad way to start the camping experience.

"Young lady, get—on—the—bus!"

Ooh. The dreaded slow hiss of instructions. This was war. My blood was almost boiling in my veins. I stared her down a few seconds more, and then I said, "Not that I doubt your leadership skills or anything, but your priority should be the lost people. Why are we not searching for them?"

Guitar Lady's face flushed red. "*We* are handling it."

"Shelby!" Jenna tugged on my sleeve. "*Get* on the bus," she said out of the corner of her mouth while smiling at Guitar Lady. She pulled me toward the luggage, but I could feel the evil musician's glare burning the back of my head.

"Arguing with the adults is not the way to make a good first impression," said Jenna, struggling to get her cases out from under some other bags. "You really want to be labeled a troublemaker?"

"No, but what about—"

"Trust me. You don't want that label," said Jenna, pulling her bag onto its wheels and rolling away. "Not at brat camp."

Ariel, who'd been standing alongside me the entire time, seemed to be the only other person truly concerned about Charles and Austin. "Do you think they'll be all right?" she asked as we finally grabbed our bags from the broken-down bus's luggage compartment. "You know, forbidden forest and all that? People don't come back from dark places like that." Little tears welled in the corners of her eyes, surprising me. I had her pegged for more of a cynic.

"Don't worry. Mr. Winters seems like . . ." Ugh. I trailed off, not believing what I was saying. Mr. Winters didn't look like he could find his way out of a 7-Eleven. I probably had a better sense of direction than that old coot. "I'm sure he'll find them," I said lamely.

Ariel dabbed at her wet eyes like she was embarrassed I'd noticed. "I hope he does."

My stomach got that queasy feeling again. What if Winters didn't find those stupid boys? I glanced over at Guitar Lady— she was smiling insanely again, helping kids onto the brat camp bus like she was taking them to Disneyland.

"This is so dumb." I set down my suitcase and zipped up my sweatshirt. "Stay here." And with that, I plunged into the dark forest.

I didn't have a compass. That thought struck me the moment Guitar Lady's voice yelling for me to come back faded in the distance. I didn't have a plan, a map, water, or food. Nothing. But if Guitar Lady hadn't been such a twit, and if I hadn't been so confident about my being good in the woods, maybe I wouldn't have dashed in there in the first place. I totally wouldn't have run . . . off.

Uh-oh.

The full impact of what I'd done hit me like a splot of bird crap. Yes, Guitar Lady had pissed me off, but I was standing in the woods at that very moment because I was trying to help some idiot boys. And I was now going to be labeled a trouble-maker. Great. I was probably only hours away from deportation to Red Canyon boot camp.

Why did those guys have to run off in the first place? I'd totally messed up because of their stupidity. Not to mention Guitar Lady, who if she knew anything about the forest at all would have called in some stinking choppers or something.

I rounded a stand of pine trees and looked back in the direction of the bus. *I should go back.* But I'd been walking for a while. Even if the bus was still there . . . I was so in trouble. But maybe if I found the boys it would redeem my running off. And if I saved chubby Mr. Winters from sure starvation and lost-in-the-forest panic, maybe I'd come away with a warning. I decided to go on.

Remembering some of the tracking stuff my dad had taught me when we'd been camping, I followed sticks broken at about knee height and quickened my pace on the brushy trail. It looked like someone had definitely gone this way. But after a while, the trail petered out. I couldn't see where the person had gone off, and there were no more broken twigs to follow. Frustrated, I paused against the trunk of a giant cedar, catching my breath.

Wait. The sound of running water. A stream? A river? I was willing to bet one of the guys would have headed toward the sound. You had to have a water source to survive in the wilderness. Oh, man. The sound was going to make me pee! I tried not to think about it and pushed my way through bushes and snaggy tree branches, glad for the protection of my sweatshirt.

Ahead of me, the path continued through a thicket of blackberries. There didn't seem to be a way around. I'd need a big stick to swack the vines. Turning around to search the sides of the trail, I saw a likely branch. I took three steps forward.

Snap!

I froze, looking down. No branch under my foot. Someone or something was close by.

"Hello?" I yelled.

A few crows flew off branches overhead.

I let out a little sigh of thankfulness. Birds. I went back to looking for a stick, laughing at myself for being so jumpy. Then I heard a growling sound.

Ariel's stories about the forbidden forest flashed through my mind as I scanned the ferns, evergreens, and bushes ahead. Holy crap. What if she was right? What if something was lurking in the brush ready to pounce? My gaze traced over the dense foliage, but nothing moved. I let out the breath I'd been holding.

The growling started again, sounding closer.

Crap. Something *was* following me. Something that thought I looked delicious and didn't know about my bladder issues. I was so dead. I was going to literally pee my pants and die. Or be eaten—which is totally worse.

The thing growled again, meaner this time.

Forcing myself to look, I swiveled my head to the right. The bushes were swaying. That I could almost handle, but then something brown darted between two huge tree trunks. An animal. A coyote? A cougar?

Suddenly, my search for a stick seemed like a really good idea. A big stick to whack that wild animal on the head before it shredded me. Without taking my eyes off the tree trunks, I lowered myself, my hands feeling around for any kind of sticklike materials. My right hand hit a loose-barked branch about the thickness of a rolling pin. Perfect. I rose up from the ground.

"*Psst!* Don't make any sudden moves!" a voice said.

I spun around and saw Mr. Winters. One front pocket of his khaki shorts was ripped open, and two scratches leaked blood down one of his pudgy calves. His face, already pasty white, now looked positively drained of color.

He raised a finger to his lips to quiet me and pointed into the blackberry thicket. "Easy, fella. We're leaving now."

Whatever was growling didn't move, but the sound intensified, raising pricklies on the back of my neck. I took a few steps backward. And then a few more.

That's when I fell down the bank.

The sliding wasn't so bad. It was the landing on the rocks that really hurt.

When I stopped moving, I was spread-eagled on two boulders overlooking a whitewater river that you probably needed a helmet to go wading in. I glanced up to the top of the cliff where I'd fallen. It was so densely covered with bushes, trees, and brambles, I couldn't see where I'd stepped off or Mr. Winters.

I struggled to my hands and knees and crawled off the boulders, onto the beach. My shorts were loaded with dirt and pebbles from my slide. Ick. I winced doing a little de-dirting shake. Double ick. The amount of soil that fell could have potted a rosebush.

Nothing on my body seemed broken, but I was incredibly sore. Scratches and raised welts streaked the backs of my thighs. And I still had to use the forest's ladies' room.

I stumbled over to the nearest tree, about twenty feet away, and dropped those dirty shorts. No sooner was I zipping up after the best pee of my life than I heard footsteps crunching on the beach. Human footsteps. Maybe Winters had found a way down the hill. Good. One out of three rescues was complete.

I peered out around the branches of the evergreen, expecting to see the old guy but found Austin in front of my tree, a half smile on his face. He looked perfectly at home against the backdrop of the river. His dark hair waved in the light breeze, and his eyes shined golden in the sunlight. For a city boy, he looked almost at one with nature.

I stepped out. "Hey! Do you know how much trouble you guys have got me into? You had no business running off into the woods."

"Shelby, wasn't it? Lovely to see you, too," he replied, the smile morphing into a smirk.

"Yeah, so lovely I'll probably be shipped off to the lower level of hell the minute we get back to camp. You could have been killed—there's a freaking wild animal up on that bluff above us! If I hadn't slid down here I would have been dinner!"

Austin's gaze traveled down my body. "So that's why you look like a garden trowel."

"A what?"

"You're filthy."

So much for British charm. I glared at him. "Mr. Winters is probably some cougar's snack right now. The last thing I'm worried about is looking good. Let's find those other idiots and get back to the bus, okay?"

"Right." Austin scratched at the back of his neck. "I tracked Charles to a ravine, but then I lost him."

"Tracked him?"

Austin's cheeks pinked up for some reason. "You know, broken twigs, footprints, that sort of thing."

"So you do know something about the woods," I said.

"A bit." Austin held a hand up to his eyes, shielding them from the sun sinking in the distance. "We've about two hours of light remaining. We need to keep searching." He turned and started up the beach again.

I marched after him. "We need to hike back to the road. Things are only going to get worse if we stay out here."

Austin shook his head. "I'm not leaving until I find Charles. And what he took."

"So it *was* your backpack—great reason to get lost in the

woods." I fought the urge to punch him on the arm. "Dude, what's in your stupid bag, gold or something?"

"You'd be surprised," he said with a grim smile.

We hiked the shoreline of the river, searching for Charles with no luck, and we couldn't scale the cliff to find Mr. Winters, but at least we didn't hear any screaming. Then again, the human voice can only carry so far.

Finally, when the sun was sinking behind the hills on the other side of the river, leaving streaks of red and orange in the sky, we gave up. It had to be about nine o'clock, judging by the growls coming from my stomach and the cheerful flock of mosquitoes beginning to circle my head. In the distance rose the pale face of the nearly full moon.

Geez, what if we were here all night? We didn't have a tent, we didn't have food, and I didn't have any toothpaste. Ick. I mean, I was all for survival, but you were supposed to have basic stuff. We had nada. Well, except for the matches in Austin's pocket, which somehow he must have thought were okay to bring to brat camp. I was pretty sure that had to be on the list of no-no's along with my beloved PDA.

As Austin piled little sticks into a makeshift fire pit, I stared out at the dying sunset and thought of my friends partying in Cabo at this very moment, probably dancing with some hunky guys. And here I was, on a rock in the middle of nowhere with a guy who'd only said three words in the past hour. My gaze drifted up to the darkening sky.

"I think I see the first star tonight," I said. "Maybe I can wish myself away from here."

"Not bloody likely," Austin said, stuffing his contraband matches into his pocket. "Wishing is a waste of time. Or so I've found." He blew on the smoldering twigs, trying to get the fire going.

I gazed down at the dark swirls in the water below my rock, watching the current rush between the stones. I hadn't been near a river in ages, and the sound of it reminded me of just how different my life was from the quiet times Dad and Mom and I had spent in the suburbs of Milwaukee. I missed camping with them in the north woods and even riding my bike in the cul-de-sacs near my house when I was little. It hadn't been flashy, but it'd been peaceful. And it had all disappeared so easily when Mom got sick. I wrapped my arms around my legs, feeling the chill of the evening and the coldness of the rock beneath me.

"You look far away," Austin said. "What are you thinking about?"

I put on a smile. "Um, just thinking about home."

"You miss it, even though your parents sent you here?" Austin asked.

"Yeah, my parents . . ." I let the sentence trail away, not wanting to finish the thought.

"They aren't always what we hope they'd be," Austin said, and his expression softened.

I nodded. "And apparently neither are we," I said.

Austin laughed. "That's true. But you can't choose your family."

"Right. Because I'm sure my dad would have picked differently," I said, only half kidding.

"Now I very much doubt that," Austin said. "My father, on the other hand, would have picked a son with a thirst for the hunt."

"What?"

Austin colored slightly. "I mean, he's on safari with my uncle right now, but that's not my cup of tea. I'd rather sketch animals than kill them for sport."

"Oh, so you're an artist?"

"I draw a little."

"Uh . . . that's art."

"Not to my father. He'd rather I play the guitar." Austin sighed and added a few more sticks to the fire. I kind of got what he was saying. I'm sure my own dad wished I was a chemistry prodigy who could follow in his footsteps.

"It must be weird having such a famous dad," I said.

Austin gave me a half smile. "Try *infamous*. But he's all I have."

"You don't have other family?"

"Just my uncle . . . and there's the entourage, if you can call them family. I spend more time with them than I do my father," he said with a little laugh. "It's hardly normal."

"Normal's overrated," I said with a shrug. "Or so I've heard."

Austin smiled broadly. With the dying sunset highlighting his strong profile, I couldn't deny it—he was cuter than I had first thought. Oh. I was totally staring at him. And he was staring back at me.

There was this weird, awkward pause, and then he cleared his throat. "You're undoubtedly cold. Perhaps I'll just . . ." he mumbled, turning back to the smoky little blaze.

I moved closer and sat on a log near the fire, watching him work. Maybe it was just the accent, or maybe he was seeming cuter because this was the closest I'd been to a boy since the night in the garden with Josh. My love life had been completely boy-free since the moment Priscilla rolled out the camp brochures. That was it. Boy deprivation.

"Shelby? Oi! Would you mind finding some twigs?" said Austin, waving his hand in front of my face to get my attention. "This fire needs fuel."

I stood up, glad for a task to take my wandering mind off Austin. "Okay. I'll look around," I said. "It's a little dark so it might take a while."

"You could use my flashlight!" came a call from down the beach.

Startled, Austin and I looked up. Mr. Winters was leading Charles toward us. Charles dragged a backpack in the sand behind him.

"Hello, lovebirds! What were you doing out here all alone in the dark?" Charles said.

"We're *not* lovebirds!" Austin and I both yelled at the same time. Then we gave each other a sorry look, realizing we'd jinxed.

"What were you two thinking?" said Mr. Winters, limping toward us. "What in heaven's name got into you kids?"

Austin said, "I was after Charles."

"And I chased after Austin, because . . . well, it's a long story," I added.

"Well, good intentions or not, you're both in hot water," said Mr. Winters, huffing up to the log and sitting down with an audible sigh.

Charles smiled broadly at me. A big gloating ha-ha smile.

That did it. "What about *him*? Charles is a thief!" I snapped. "He took Austin's stuff."

"And how does that involve you?" asked Mr. Winters.

"Oh." I chewed my lip for a half sec. "Well, honestly, I was just trying to help find them because that crazy Guitar Lady wasn't doing jack."

Mr. Winters gave me a thoughtful look, and then said, "We'll sort it out back at camp. Put out the fire. We'll use my GPS to find our way back to the road and then I can radio for the camp van." He rose shakily to his feet and took a few steps, wincing. "Let's go. The cook's making the best blueberry cobbler you ever tasted and we're missing it."

"Blueberry cobbler?" said Charles. "Yumm-o. I can't wait to get to camp." He was suddenly all calm, and that completely irked me.

45

"First things first. *You* can give Austin his stuff back now," I said, yanking the black backpack from Charles's hands.

"Not so fast. How do you know it's his?" said Charles, jerking the bag back by the zipper pull.

"Hand it here." Austin reached for it just as Charles let go.

In the struggle something tumbled out of the backpack, clinking like glass on glass. Mr. Winters's flashlight beam zoomed to a bunch of clear vials rolling into a loose pile in the sand.

People probably try to smuggle booze into camps like this, but the vials held less than a swallow. They were even smaller than bottles from a hotel mini-bar. Maybe they weren't alcohol at all. Oh, man, I'd found out the reason he was here—British bad boy had a drug problem. I didn't know what to say. I just stood staring at the glittering pile.

Austin tried to scoop his vials up discreetly, but Mr. Winters hobbled over and stood over him with his hand out. Ignoring the old man, Austin went on collecting the vials and placing them in a plastic bag.

"Austin, give me your backpack," Mr. Winters said. "We would have confiscated your stash at camp anyway."

"It's not what you think. This is a prescription," Austin replied, hugging the pack to his chest.

"A prescription?" Charles chuckled. "I don't know about that. I drank one of those an hour ago and I feel pretty buzzed."

"You drank one of my doses? Are you daft?" Austin stepped closer to Charles, looking ready to knock him out.

Charles smiled defiantly. "If the old man hadn't shown up, I would have had more."

"Charles! Start throwing dirt on the fire," Mr. Winters snapped, and then turned to Austin. "Son, when we get back to camp, we'll phone your father and sort this problem out."

Austin kicked a rock into the smoldering fire. "You can't ring him up," he said.

Mr. Winters shook his head as if he'd heard it all before. "I'm sure there's a way."

Austin bit his lower lip. "He's on holiday in remote Africa. No phones. No television. No contact."

"Of course." Mr. Winters sounded unconvinced. "Well, if it is prescribed, it'll be on your medical form in the camp records."

"What about his manager?" I said, trying to be helpful. "I mean, he has one, right?"

"Graham doesn't know anything about this," Austin hissed. "He's only just started working for the band. He'll be sacked when my father learns I was sent here instead of on holiday like I'd planned. I'm not supposed to be here at all."

There was pain in his voice. A lonely pain that made my heart squinch up a little. The guy was obviously using drugs to cover up that pain. I felt for him.

Mr. Winters seemed unfazed by Austin's story. "I'll guard this contraband, whatever it is, until we can get in touch with him," he said, taking Austin's pack and swinging it over his arms the wrong way so it rested on his belly like he was pregnant.

Austin's eyes blazed with so much anger, I thought he was going to take a swing at the old guy. Through gritted teeth he said, "I need it. You don't understand."

"It's all going to be fine," Mr. Winters said, putting an arm around Austin's shoulders. "You don't need those chemicals to feel good about yourself. We'll work on it at camp. We'll take care of you, son. Let's go, campers."

I sighed as I fell into step behind Mr. Winters and the boys. So, Austin was just another celebrity's kid hooked on drugs. I felt kinda sorry for him. I mean, I'd seen all the *Behind the Music*s about the sad lives of bands and their families. It was lonely out there on the road. But wait—normal people got lonely, too. That didn't mean you had to cover that pain with drugs.

I trudged ahead, trying to put his problem out of my mind. I had enough troubles of my own at the moment. But as we hiked through the woods by the glow of the wimpy flashlight, my thoughts kept going back to Austin. He didn't seem like a druggie. He was more together than the kids at school I knew used. He even seemed kinda smart. So how did he get into that crap? There had to be something I could do to help him. I mean, after the lame guys I'd helped with their small problems, here was a guy who obviously needed help in the worst way.

Wait! Get a grip, my brain scolded, *you're in deep doo-doo yourself!* Right. The point was to help myself. I had to remember that. *Follow the rules, do my time, stay far away from Red Canyon.*

I decided to focus on the trail ahead, which worked until Austin glanced back at me as we crested a hill. His eyes glimmered in a sliver of moonlight. And my skin prickled with goose bumps. Me. Him. The moon. I was toast.

FOUR

The sight of Camp Crescent brought camp life flooding back into my brain. The cabin cliques, the smell of apple crisp, the deformed weaving projects from arts and crafts. That feeling that no matter how much fresh air you breathed, you could never fill yourself up enough. I'd loved summer camp when I was a little kid and my parents would send me up to Camp Winnemuk or to sailing camp on Lake Michigan.

But there was one major difference at Camp Crescent. Barbed-wire fencing. From the van window, I could see it snaking around the perimeter of the property, separating Camp Crescent from the edge of the forbidden forest.

Charles noticed it, too. "That's jail-grade," he said in an awestruck voice.

Austin didn't turn from gazing out the window. He'd been silent since we'd hiked out of the woods. Even during the long wait for the camp van to show up, he hadn't said a word. Maybe he'd been trying to figure out how to get his drugs back.

I chewed my lip, replaying the whole looking-back-over-his-shoulder thing. I couldn't stop thinking about the way his eyes had reflected the light on the trail. Silvery, almost bluish, otherworldly. It was just my crappy luck the boy with the coolest eyes I'd ever seen had to be at *my* brat camp. And had to get me off to such a lame start. I mean, Mr. Winters had a GPS and a cell phone! He would have been fine without me helping out, but Austin had made me run into the woods. Totally lame.

For my own good, I focused on pushing Austin, his beautiful eyes, and his problem out of my mind. It wasn't exactly easy to do with him in the seat across from me and the faint scent of his cologne and his leather jacket in the air.

At last, the van rolled to a stop at the end of the gravel road. The three of us followed a limping Mr. Winters down a path toward a building that resembled a barn. The dining hall must have been nearby, because the smell of frying onions hung in the air. My stomach gurgled so loudly, Charles looked over at me with a smirk.

Austin put his hand on my arm, stopping me. "Shelby," he whispered, "it's not what you think. *I'm* not what you must think."

"It's okay, Austin. Everyone has their problems. You don't have to explain," I said.

Austin let out a breath. "I feel as though I should. I wouldn't want you to—"

"No dillydallying!" called Mr. Winters, waving us on before hobbling around a corner of the building with Charles.

Austin didn't budge. "Shelby, I'm not on drugs."

"Dude, I know what I saw, but whatever. I'm not here to judge." I started to walk away, but Austin grabbed my hand and pulled me into the shadows.

Again, I caught a whiff of that cologne smell and something different but yummy. I tried not to breathe it in. It was like girl kryptonite for sure. "We have to go," I said.

"My family likes its privacy. We keep to ourselves. We don't need more rumors and lies leaked out to the press. We've been through enough." He stared into my eyes, dead serious.

"I really thought guys like you had tougher skin. I mean, you actually care what some stupid reporters make up about you?"

"It's complicated," Austin said. "But I don't want you to think the wrong thing about me."

"Why would you care what I think? I mean, you don't even know me."

"No." A sad look flickered in his eyes. "In the woods I thought that you . . . and I . . ."

"Oh. Ohhhh." I sucked in a breath. So this was the moonlight-magic-look talk. This was the part where I got to be all "I don't date drug-crazed hotties who will get me sent to boot camp." Wait. Crap. I was probably already on my way there. "Look, I know what it's like to crush on someone, but we just met and—"

"In the woods it seemed like we might become friends," he said, finishing his thought.

Eek. My face felt like it was on fire. "Uh-huh."

"I can't have a friend believing rubbish about me."

"No, of course not," I said, discreetly trying to fan my cheeks. I took a deep breath and fixed him with a stare. "So, *friend*, what was in those vials?"

"Truthfully, a prescription. Badly needed medicine."

I rolled my eyes. "Yeah, you said that already. So, what's it for?"

Austin raked his teeth over his bottom lip. "Ah, that's the difficult part." Austin leveled his gaze at mine, like he was trying to think of how to say something important. Something flickered in his eyes. Some strange trick of the light that made goose bumps prickle on my neck.

"Campers! What is going on?" Mr. Winters called, coming back around the corner of the building. "I told you two no dilly-dallying."

"We're coming," said Austin.

Mr. Winters frowned. "Shelby? Are you all right?"

"Huh?" I murmured, still trying to figure out what I'd seen flash in Austin's eyes. It'd been different from the trail. Almost dangerous.

"Shelby?" Mr. Winters repeated.

I blinked at him. "Oh. Um, I'm on my way."

"Believe me," Austin whispered in my ear as he passed.

‹‹‹

Mr. Winters led us into a wood-paneled room decorated with brass animal sculptures and stuffed fish trophies. A huge desk with legs carved like talons gripping balls stood inside the door. I'm not into antique stuff or anything, but that piece alone had to be worth major cash. On the corner of the desk a brass eagle statue perched, as if it were about to take flight.

Guitar Lady looked up as we walked in. Fortunately, there was no sign of her freaking instrument. That was enough to make me smile, though at any second she would probably whip out a harmonica from her pocket. In addition to the flowery summer dress she'd had on earlier, she now wore an old-lady crocheted cape thing and a straw safari hat. She reminded me of one of those zookeepers who always come on talk shows with three-toed sloths that pee on the host's desk. Clueless, peed on, and smiling fakely all the while.

Next to her on the red leather couch sat a golden-haired guy in a tight-fitting tracksuit who was either a counselor or a personal trainer who'd been working out way too much. He smiled at us so brightly, I could almost hear his teeth go *ping*.

We three runaways sat down on an identical couch opposite the adults, me between the two boys. I prepared myself to hear the lecture of a lifetime, sure I was headed for that brat camp in the desert. Had I packed enough sunscreen?

Mr. Winters plunked down into the high-backed chair at the desk, his head level with a gaping bass trophy. The fish's eyes, little glassy beads, stared out, eerily similar to Mr. Winters's own. "Campers," he began, "first, I'd like to introduce Cynthia Crumb and Sven Jorgensen. Shelby, you'll be in Cynthia's cabin—Spotted Owl. Charles and Austin, I've assigned you to Sven's Sapsucker."

Charles snorted. "Sapsucker?"

"That's a kind of bird," explained Sven with another blinding smile and an accent thicker than the dude's on the IKEA commercials. "Very nice bird."

Charles gave Sven a dorky salute. Austin didn't even look up, he just nodded, his dark hair falling into his eyes.

"Campers, you'll meet me tomorrow after breakfast. While everyone else is trying their hand at archery, we'll be discussing your wandering and working out your restitution. Cynthia, Sven, these folks'll see you back at the cabins."

Wait. That was it? No Red Canyon? "You're not calling my parents?" My hope-filled heart did a little cartwheel. This doughy camp director was a total walk in the park compared to evil Priscilla.

"Shelby, we operate on a second-chance basis here," Mr. Winters said. "We will be calling your parents tomorrow morning. However, I expect they'll let you continue the program on our advice."

"Oh." My hopes crashed with a thud. So, Dad and Priscilla would find out about the unauthorized forest field trip. That was not going to look good.

"Now then, you kids must be hungry. I'm sure the cook managed to save us a few plates." He patted his belly, which made me realize he was the one who was completely starving.

Then again, when you're eating for two—you and your beer gut—you probably get that starving feeling a lot.

Anyway, we all rose from the couches and followed him to the door.

"What was that about restitution?" said Charles. "If you let me use your phone, I'll wire cash directly into your account." He flicked a piece of bark off his polo shirt; it landed on Austin's shoe.

Mr. Winters stopped in the doorway and turned, his eyebrows furrowed. "Phones are secured for staff only, and we *work* things off here, Charles. Kitchen cleanup duty, pulling weeds, that sort of thing. Also, for the time being, you won't be able to participate in the trail building we're doing on the west side of the boundary."

Austin seemed to perk up, raising his eyes to Mr. Winters for the first time since we'd been in the room. "Trail building?" he repeated.

"A privilege, for respected campers, son."

Sven grinned again. "You like to build trails, Austin?"

Austin shrugged, the light in his eyes dimming.

"How about you?" asked Cynthia, her gaze sweeping over me and my filthy clothes. "Handy with a shovel?"

I nodded. "My stepmom has prize rosebushes."

Cynthia shared a look with Mr. Winters, like she couldn't believe I'd ever set foot in a flower bed. "Your gardener's work, no doubt."

"How do you know?" I replied, because I didn't like the tone of her comment. Was she one of those people who thought everyone who had money was lazy? If only she knew just a few years ago I'd been lucky to scrape together enough cash for the movies.

"Fine, fine. We've all got gardeners. Where's dinner?" Charles said, pushing past the adults to the doorway.

"Hungry boy, this one," said Sven, clapping Charles on the back. "We'll feed you now." He wrapped a beefy arm around Charles's skinny shoulders and marched him out the door. "You come, Shelby," called Sven over his shoulder.

Cynthia adjusted her crocheted wrap.

I took a step away, in case she was about to put her arm around me. I didn't need a snotty middle-aged lady with guitar issues trying to be my friend. I said, "I'll, um, find my own way."

Her tight smile practically screamed for ChapStick. "See you at Spotted Owl," she said, then stalked off, humming.

"Shall we?" asked Austin, holding the door for me.

"Oh, um . . . thanks." I let myself breathe a sigh of relief as I stepped out into the night air and toward the smell of food.

Austin walked beside me, and there was this comfortable silence between us, at least until we entered the dining hall and heard Charles trying to send back his overcooked pork chop. Yep. I was definitely at brat camp.

After our late dinner, I was looking forward to settling into my cabin—until I heard a guitar strumming out a verse of "Michael, Row the Boat Ashore." Groaning, I followed the sound to the end of the trail. Stuck in a grove of tall evergreens, Spotted Owl, like the seven or so other cabins I had passed, was made of fake siding rounded to look like logs. So much for rustic.

I paused on the doorstep and looked back down the dark trail to where Austin was easing through the lighted doorway of Sapsucker. He hadn't said much during dinner, but our whispered conversation on the path earlier still haunted me. He thought of me as a friend. And I thought of him as a cute guy. A cute guy with big problems.

Sighing, I inched open the door to Spotted Owl. On a single bed near the entrance, Cynthia Crumb was rockin' out on her guitar, while the girls in the bunk beds all around the room looked bored, annoyed, or had pillows over their heads. I stood there in the doorway until the song ended and then, thankfully, Cynthia packed up her so-called instrument.

I eased into the room and took the first empty lower bunk.

"Hey," said a voice in the next bed. Two brown eyes and a mess of black hair emerged from beneath a pillow. Ariel. I'd never been so happy to see a familiar face. I took a quick look around, wondering if Jenna had been stuck here, too, but I didn't see her.

"I thought you died out there," said Ariel, scooching over onto my bunk.

"Huh? I was trying to save Austin's butt. You really know him?"

"Yeah," said Ariel, brushing her hair out of her face. "My dad's friends with his dad. Talk about a wild old guy."

"Shelby?" Cynthia interrupted, sticking her pinched-up face in mine. "Go get your suitcase. I need to search it."

"Huh? You need to *what*?"

"Standard procedure," said Cynthia in a bored voice. "Your bag is waiting on the porch. I'm surprised you didn't trip over it."

"You've got to be kidding. What happened to the Bill of Rights? Am I not entitled to a little privacy and respect?"

Cynthia smiled like a shark. "While I understand your concern, your parents were happy enough to sign your rights away. Move it."

"C'mon, I'll help you," said Ariel, springing up. Once we were outside, Ariel whispered, "She's pure evil. Stay on her good side."

"And here I thought she hated me because I don't sing stupid songs."

"She probably hates everyone for that," Ariel said with a laugh.

"So, um . . . what else do you know about Austin Bridges?"

"What?" Ariel's eyes got bigger, which seemed impossible considering the size of them to begin with. "Do you like him?"

"No. I mean, I just met him. He seems interesting."

Ariel raised her eyebrows. "Well, actually, I don't know Austin all that well. His dad tours without him usually."

"Oh. That's too bad. Austin probably misses him."

"Nah, he's probably fine. I mean, I hardly ever see my parentals." Ariel shrugged. "I'm doing okay. Well, except for being sent to brat camp every summer. Why are you so worried about him, anyway?"

I didn't want to say anything about what had happened in the woods. And I really didn't want to gossip about Austin's problem. "He seems sad," I said, and let the subject drop.

Ariel and I dragged my suitcase into the cabin and threw it onto my bed. My bunkmates gathered around as Cynthia picked through my suitcase with pleasure.

"Contraband can be hidden anywhere," she said, separating my underwear with a pencil. Yeah, contraband—as in my stash of gummy worms (for those extra-bad days), lip gloss, and my favorite glitter eye shadow.

She pitched those remnants of civilization into a plastic bag. "And I'll be taking this Wonderbra," she said, hooking her pencil in a strap. "You're supposed to be concentrating on bettering yourself, not trying to attract male attention."

"You've got to be kidding!" I said.

Cynthia smoothed a strand of her gray-blond bobbed hair back behind one ear. "Not in the least," she said in a bored voice. "Push-up bras are strictly prohibited."

The other girl campers murmured to each other.

"C'mon, guys," I said. "I can't be the only one who brought along a little cleavage enhancement."

A skinny blond girl in braces nodded her head sadly. "I'm really gonna miss my La Perla T-shirt bra."

Cynthia continued her inspection, now pawing through my backpack. Scowling, she picked up my romance paperback and then tucked it under her arm.

"Hold it," I complained. "Reading can't be a distraction. You'd think camp would try to enhance our education."

Cynthia tied a knot at the top of her bag of my goodies and swung it over her shoulder like a true Grinch. "Shelby, everyone knows those books are trashy."

My mouth dropped open.

A pretty dark-haired girl in the bunk above me said, "No they're not! My mom's made a million writing those kinds of books."

Cynthia shot her a death glare and then stomped to the front of the cabin. "I'm going to have Mr. Winters lock this stuff up. When I get back it's lights out," she said, closing the door behind her.

"Hey, don't feel bad. She took all of my prototypes for the DeVoisier spring line," Ariel told me. "Five shades of lavender shadow, two plum lip glosses, and a pot of peachy cheek stain."

"You wear that much makeup?"

Ariel shook her head. "Sympathy present from my mother for sending me away."

"We're all supposed to look like crap," said the romance girl from the top bunk. "They say it's therapeutic."

"Great." I started refolding my violated stuff, feeling as low as I had since I'd first boarded the plane back in LA. No push-up bra, no eye shadow, no candy. I couldn't imagine that things could get worse. But of course they did.

FIVE

Claaaannnnnggg! Someone's alarm clock really needed to die. I sat up in bed, covering my ears with my hands. Even then I could still hear it loud and clear. It wasn't coming from our cabin at all.

"Oh, crap!" shrieked the romance girl. "Are we on fire?" She threw herself over the side of her top bunk, managing to kick me in the head on the way down.

"Ahh!" I screamed, now fully awake. "Watch it, Sara!"

Ariel peeked out from under her pillow. "Stupid camp!" she moaned. "Why don't they let us sleep?"

"Don't ask me. I've probably got brain damage." I rubbed my forehead.

"Let's go, let's go, Spotted Owl!" shouted Cynthia Crumb. The bell had been ringing for two minutes already, the cabin was in panic mode, and she just now shot out of bed. After swatting at her tangled hair, she threw jeans on over her dorky flannel nightgown and then ran around the cabin like some kind of goat herder or something. "Put a shirt over that tank," she told a tiny blond girl, and then moved on to the next slow-poke. "Brenna, get your butt out of bed! Let's go! It's a drill! We're being timed!" she squawked in my ear. "Report to the flagpole! Move it! Move it!"

"Man, she scares me," whispered Ariel after Cynthia marched away.

We were the last ones out of the cabin since I had to find a missing sandal and Ariel had to pee. We hustled up to the lawn in front of the dining hall only to find all the other campers loosely bunched in a circle.

I saw Austin on the fringe of the Sapsucker crowd. He was wearing jeans and a black T-shirt and had an incredibly bored look on his face. As Ariel and I approached, Austin raised his eyebrows slightly and gave me a little nod.

I gave him a half smile as Ariel tugged my hand and pulled me toward Cynthia and the girls.

"Well, campers . . ." Up near the flagpole, Mr. Winters spoke into a microphone. "It seems Spotted Owl is bringing up the rear this morning. We'll need to work on that emergency response system for next time."

Red-faced, Ariel and I slipped in behind the rest of our group. Cynthia turned to give us a disapproving look.

"So, as I was saying," Mr. Winters said, "we have a number of wonderful projects planned for you folks in the weeks ahead: horseback riding, trail building, square dancing, and the ever-popular talent show, to name a few. Today some of you will summit Crescent Rock for the first time."

Ariel gasped. "I so don't do heights," she said in a zombie-like tone.

I gave her a pat on the back.

"And, campers, one of the highlights of Camp Crescent is our Transformation Ceremony, which will happen at the end of this week. You'll be doing an art project, a representation of the person you used to be, of the things you'd like to change about yourself, and releasing it into the fire under the full moon. With that vision of yourself gone, you'll be able to find the real you, the authentic person you'd like to become."

I grimaced. That sounded a little more woo-woo than the brochure. I was all for transforming, but burning an effigy in a campfire? That was pretty out there. Still, I listened to him describe the daily routine, and looked at all the faces of the campers around the clumpy circle we formed on the lawn. I thought maybe it wouldn't be all that different from regular camp. Maybe it'd almost be fun. But maybe is never a sure thing.

"Let's talk about your stepmother," Mr. Winters said, handing me a pair of gardening gloves later that morning.

I braced myself against the rock wall surrounding the flower bed. It was one thing to be paying a penalty for running off, but did it have to come with extra therapy? Just an hour ago, I'd been to a "girls' group," where a chubby psychologist named Dr. Wanda had asked each of us to describe how we felt when we had our first period. Ugh. Listening to that was torture enough.

"Mr. Winters, could you just show me what you want weeded?" I said. I shaded my eyes against the bright morning sun and gave him my best shut-it look. Of course, he kept standing there, his belly making some impressive shade.

I really hoped he wasn't one of those annoying adults who think that silence is the guaranteed way to make kids talk. I'd seen enough counselors fail with that old tactic.

When my mom died, there were things I couldn't talk about—especially to the therapists Dad had set me up with. I didn't even know how I was feeling then, and I really didn't want to talk to strangers. I mean, I couldn't even talk about stuff to my own dad. And so those random professionals had wasted Dad's money staring at me across a desk, appointment after appointment. And eventually my dad gave up on the counselor idea. Then he found Honey Bun and forgot about it, and everything else, completely.

Yeah, I'd seen Mr. Winters's type before.

After a moment of my silence, Mr. Winters gave in and said, "Let's talk some more about your running away from camp."

I blinked at him. Hadn't we been over this already? "I was worried about the guys and you. I thought I could help."

"Helping is a good thing—when you can do it safely."

"Yeah," I said, bracing myself for the rest of the lecture.

From the nearby field, another wave of laughing and talking rose from the kids enjoying archery. I glanced in that direction and noticed Austin and Charles across the gravel road, stacking rocks to form another landscaping wall. Already sweating, both the boys had their shirts off. Austin's muscular chest gleamed in the sunlight. Mmm.

Mr. Winters tracked my gaze and said, "What does Austin represent to you? A dangerous male? A way to rebel?"

Oh, geez, my bad. For a second I'd forgotten the old guy was there with me. "Do we have to talk, Mr. Winters? See, I'm pulling a weed," I said, ripping at something green. "I can totally do this on my own."

Mr. Winters dropped to his knees. "That's a sunflower sprout," he said, stilling my hand.

"Fine." I dropped the torn leaves and sat back on my heels. "Show me what to pull then."

"Shelby," Mr. Winters said, adjusting the straw gardening hat that covered his balding head. "Attraction to boys is part of growing up."

"Attraction? Who said anything about that?"

Mr. Winters waved away a bee that circled the bright red band on his hat. "Why else would you have gone into the woods after Austin?"

"I didn't mean to go after him, but no one was doing anything, and I'm probably the only one here who's actually been in the woods for real," I said. "Besides—he's British. What do they know about camping and wilderness survival and all that?" I said, exasperated. "They're too busy drinking tea and playing cricket. He would have been lost without me." Okay, so that was a little thick, but I wanted Mr. Winters to let me pull my weeds in peace.

"Hm . . . interesting." He gave me a small smile. "Responsibility is a powerful draw, but not as powerful as sexual attraction."

"What? Can we just pull some weeds now? Please?" My skin felt all scratchy and prickly, and I didn't think it was from the plants. Mr. Winters mentioning sex was even worse than the birds-and-bees talk my dad had tried to give me last year. At least then I could explain that the schools had already taught me all I needed to know in fifth grade. "Tell me, is there a weed anywhere in this flower bed?"

Mr. Winters pointed at a clump of ugly-looking green fronds, and I yanked them out of the dirt. "Let's go back to your stepmother," he said in a smooth voice.

"Her again?"

Mr. Winters took the weed from my hand and set it in the small pile by his fat knees. "She said this kind of problem with the opposite sex is what got you into trouble in the past."

"She said that?" I scratched at my elbow with one of my gloved hands, in the process smearing dirt on my arm.

"She told me a lot of things," Mr. Winters said.

"My problem is not boys," I said, dabbing at my arm with the hem of my baby T.

"Oh no?" he replied. "It's not boys?"

"No. But she would say that."

"Tell me why you think you're here."

"Because Priscilla is evil?" I muttered.

Mr. Winters smiled sadly. "Unless you open up, you'll have trouble here at Camp Crescent, Shelby."

"Maybe I don't want to open up," I said, searching the ground around me for more weeds.

"Your stepmother seemed very concerned about you when we spoke this morning," Mr. Winters said.

I glanced up sharply. "She mentioned Red Canyon, didn't she?"

He nodded. "How does that make you feel?"

What? Was he serious? "Uh, I'm not a fan."

"I can assure you, you'll enjoy Camp Crescent much better. You don't want to jeopardize your time here."

Despite the warm sun overhead, I felt a chill, as if Priscilla stood behind me, blocking the rays. "I'll try," I said in a small voice. "You know, to open up and stuff."

"Good." Mr. Winters hoisted himself to his feet, dusting his hands off on his jeans. "And I want to suggest that you think about putting yourself first, instead of worrying about other people. Austin has his own problems to deal with. And you are the most important person in your life. You can't help other people if you don't help yourself first."

"Yeah." I grubbed around in the dirt for another weed to pull. "Sure, that's probably good advice."

"We'll talk more tomorrow," Mr. Winters said. He reached down to pat my shoulder and added, "When you hear the lunch bell, you can stop weeding for today."

Hours later, I looked up from my patch of dirt, which was now nearly weed-free. Surprisingly, that tiny accomplishment actually made me feel a little good. It'd been a long, long time since I'd pulled weeds. Back in Wisconsin, before Re-Gen, I'd helped my parents with all kinds of yard work. Mom had especially loved planting and watching things grow.

I sat back on my heels and glanced over at the guys. Apparently, Mr. Winters had told them to put their shirts back on. In his black T, Austin must have been sweating big-time, but he looked like it didn't bother him. Charles, on the other hand, appeared about ready to wilt like a daisy. He plunked down on the grass while Austin heaved another rock onto the decorative wall.

Austin saw me watching him. He gazed back at me, his eyes glinting golden in the sunlight. A little shiver traveled down the back of my neck. Those eyes were dangerous.

He waved, as if he expected me to come over, but I didn't. I looked down at the dirt patch in front of me, pretending to look for more weeds. I didn't want to get involved with anyone who might get me sent to Red Canyon. Not that the old guy was right or anything, but I did need to concentrate on helping myself at the moment.

Still, I felt bad for Austin. I could only imagine what it must be like to be the son of a rock star, raised by hired people and not by your own dad. That had to hurt. And he was right— something about talking with him in the woods had been kinda cool. In our brief conversation, I'd almost felt like we understood each other somehow.

I looked back over my shoulder at Austin, expecting to see him still watching me, but he'd gone back to building his wall.

That was about the saddest thing I'd seen him do yet.

SIX

"Shelby, you missed all the fun!" squealed Jenna, sliding into the seat next to me at lunch. She'd been assigned to the Muskrat cabin, according to Ariel, but still seemed to think we were going to be BFF. Not to be mean or anything, but she was starting to get on my nerves.

In fact, several of the people were starting to get on my nerves. So far, in the line for lunch, I'd learned about somebody hooking up with a counselor at some other camp last year, listened to someone cheerfully describe their mother's shopping addiction, and heard someone else speculate about Cynthia Crumb's personal life. I'm sure the other kids were nice and all, but so far I was starting to feel like Ariel was the only one worth hanging out with.

"I totally rocked archery," Jenna continued. She slipped her paper napkin onto her lap, covering the bright pink shorts that matched her tank printed with butterflies. "I almost got two bull's-eyes this morning," she said, bubbling over. "Can you even believe it?"

Ariel shot her an annoyed look. "Jenna, that's so mean. You know she was gardening."

Ignoring Ariel, Jenna frowned down at the tuna casserole on her tray. "Disgusting. Well, anyway, archery was super fun. You would have liked it."

"Yeah." I stirred the cheesy bits into the noodles, trying to disguise the grayish tuna flakes. Skeptically, I took a bite but found it tasted pretty good. Nothing like the ultra health food Priscilla had our housekeeper whip up all the time. Stuff like bulgur wheat pilaf and mushroom curry that I pretended to eat but mostly shoved in the garbage.

Ariel, sporting another dark outfit of a gray T and black shorts, stuck a fork in her blue Jell-O and shoved her tray away from her.

"Pretty gross, huh?" I said, giving her a nod. I really wanted to ask her more about Austin, but lunch surrounded by campers desperate for something to talk about was not the time.

Almost as if she was reading my mind, Jenna said, "So, Shelby—give us the dirt." Her loud voice attracted the stares of all the camper girls at our table. "You know, on Austin's little problem."

I gaped at her. "What?"

Ariel said, "Camp gossip." She dabbed at her lips with her paper napkin and then balled it in her fist. "The kind people should ignore."

Jenna opened her mouth to say something just as a woman's shout echoed through the packed dining room.

"Mr. Winters!" Cynthia charged through the dining hall door, tugging Austin by the arm.

"This is ridiculous," Austin said, shrugging out of Cynthia's grasp.

Mr. Winters rushed up to handle the situation. Well, *rushed* isn't exactly the word. *Limped in a hurry* is more like it. "What's going on, Cynthia?"

"I caught this boy hanging around the office." She leaned in closer, but I could still hear her say, "Trying to pick the lock of your door."

Everyone at our table stopped eating.

Cynthia made a huffing noise and put her hands on her hips. "Sir, he was breaking in to steal back his stash," she said in a loud whisper.

A buzz of reaction rose up from the kids. Mr. Winters's stern gaze swept around, silencing us.

"Cynthia," he said, stepping closer to the counselor, "we'll speak about this privately."

"I should hope so!" Austin protested. "An unfair accusation . . ."

"Let's take a walk," said Mr. Winters.

As he and Cynthia marched off with Austin, the buzz took over the room again. Sven hopped up and flapped his arms around, trying to quiet the campers but really looking like he was doing aerobics, so nobody paid attention.

"Everyone knows his drugs are locked up in Winters's office," Jenna said with a wicked grin. "Along with all the other contraband they find."

"I can't believe he's into drugs," said Ariel quietly.

"Charles totally saw him," Jenna said.

"What a gossip," I muttered.

Jenna shook her head. "Shelby, don't you know? Charles's dad just acquired *Celebrities Exposed*. Charles is digging for stories so he can bargain with his dad to get out of here. He totally bragged about it at breakfast."

Ariel shook her head sadly. "A Bridges scandal would be front-page news again. Austin's dad's a freaking rock legend."

Uh-oh. I felt creepy-crawlies run up and down my arms. Great. Just what Austin was afraid of, more tabloid gossip about his family.

Jenna leaned over and whispered, "So, you were there, Shelby. What did he have?"

"I don't know," I said. "I don't want to talk about it, okay?"

"Fine. Take all the fun out of this boring old place," Jenna said, getting up with her tray. "Maybe you should work on your communication skills, Shelby."

"Maybe you should work on your drama addiction, Jenna," countered Ariel.

"Maybe you should work on your antisocial tendencies, Ariel," replied Jenna, flouncing off.

"She's guessing," Ariel said in a bored voice. "Spend enough time at these camps, you start to be able to guess why people are here."

I frowned. "My communication skills are fine," I said.

"Actually, I had you pegged for defiance issues," Ariel said with a little smile. "You communicate okay."

Bingo. I bit my lower lip. "Well, you're definitely not antisocial," I said.

"I know. I'm shy and misunderstood, but I come from a family of extroverts. That means there must be something defective with me, right?" She laughed it off, but I saw sadness in her eyes.

"Families suck," I said.

Ariel shrugged and twirled the fork in her blue Jell-O. "You want any of this crap?"

"No. I never eat anything blue."

She smiled. "Good rule."

We left the table with our trays and dumped the garbage in the trash can.

"It's okay if you don't want to talk about it, but I can't believe Austin would use drugs. He's not a partier, from what I remember," said Ariel.

"He says the drug is some kind of medicine. Would he lie about something like that?"

Ariel shrugged. "He doesn't seem like a liar. He's totally

normal—especially when you compare him to his dad. His dad's insane or something."

We stuck our trays in the pile on the counter and headed out the door.

"Insane?" I asked.

Ariel nodded, putting on her sunglasses. "Completely mental. Once, at my parents' Christmas party, I saw his dad bite the head off a parakeet," Ariel whispered as we rounded the corner of the dining hall. "A *live* parakeet."

"No way. Eww."

"Yep. Crazy old rocker dude."

"That's disgusting."

Ariel grimaced at the memory. "Austin thought so, too. He ran out of the party looking like he was totally going to puke."

"Why is his dad so crazy?"

"He's always been nuts. He's nothing like Austin."

I nodded. "Austin seems so different. Kind of sad, even."

Ariel sucked in a breath. "You don't know, do you?" she said.

"What?"

"Austin's mom died."

"She did?" Oh, man. My heart started to beat harder. I hadn't mentioned my own mom. Usually people didn't get it—what it's like to lose a parent. It's easier to let them assume my parents are divorced like everyone else's. I tried to keep my face normal while Ariel went on.

"She was shot a while ago in some kind of hunting accident in Scotland. At least that's what my parents told me."

A little shiver passed through me. Shot. No wonder Austin had problems.

"Are you okay?" Ariel asked, raising her sunglasses to scan my face. "You look really white. Like beyond-help-of-bronzer white."

I let out the breath I'd been holding. "I'm fine."

"It's shocking, I know. Could you even imagine losing your mom?" Ariel said. "I would freak."

I just nodded.

She said, "Even if you hate your mom, you know, you can't grow up without her."

Yes you can—I wanted to say, but I didn't. I didn't need Ariel feeling sorry for me. I didn't need her making imaginary connections between Austin and me just because we'd lost our moms.

Lost. Yeah, right. Why do we always say *lost* when we mean people died on us? Mom was not lost. And I'd spent the last three years trying hard not to lose myself. That's what really happens when people die—the family left behind loses a part of themselves. A tiny piece. A tiny piece you never get back.

Ariel slid her glasses back into place. "You sure you're okay?" she asked.

"Uh, yeah." I recovered a smile. "My stepmom's pretty bad. She sent me here."

"Uh-oh." Ariel stopped on the path to the cabin, putting her hand on my arm. "That happened to a friend of mine. It's a stepmother trick. Your dad totally fell for it."

"She sent me here to get rid of me. I guess I really am normal."

Ariel shrugged, and we started walking again. "You know, I don't think anyone is normal anymore," she said. "Everyone's got something weird about them. Something they think they ought to hide."

I nodded.

"Oh, look!" Ariel said, pointing at a squirrel skittering up a pine tree.

I shook my head at her. "I thought you'd been to a lot of camps—didn't you ever see a squirrel?"

She blinked at me. "My dad's apartment overlooks Central Park. I've seen squirrels before. Not that I'm a super nature girl like you. That stuff about living in Wisconsin is true, isn't it?" She lowered her sunglasses, giving me an appraising look.

"Like I'd make something like that up to impress the girls of Spotted Owl?"

"You'd be surprised at some of the stuff campers lie about." Ariel smiled. "Anyway, I like your style. What are you doing here at the 'most exclusive teen therapy facility in the West' anyway?"

I laughed at the little quote marks she was making with her fingers and said, "I'm still trying to figure that one out."

"I can't make it," wailed Ariel two hours later.

I glanced up at the massive rock wall in front of us. Handholds jutted out every few vertical feet, but even that wasn't a comfort to Ariel, who was only partway up. I tightened my hold on the rope threaded through the harness and belay device I was strapped into. From me, the rope ran to stays at the top of the rock and then down to Ariel's gear. By controlling the slack, I helped steady her while she climbed.

"Come on! You're doing really well!" I called out, trying to be a good partner. Actually, she was doing okay for someone who was afraid of heights. She'd begged the counselors to let her out of the activity, but they hadn't budged. Everyone had to take on Crescent Rock, or so they said. Conquering a natural obstacle was part of our transformation stuff.

From a platform at the top of the wall, Mr. Winters waved his hands. "You can do it, campers! Let's go."

"You're almost there, Ariel!" I yelled.

"Oi!" Austin was at the top of the pack of ten campers on the wall. He must have worked everything out with Mr. Winters from the look of things. So maybe he was doing fine all on his own. That was a relief. "Ease up on the rope, mate!"

His partner, Charles, let out more of the rope from the belay device, easing it through his guide hand, and Austin reached for the next handholds.

"Check out this fake," Charles muttered. "He acts like he's never been to a brat camp in his life. He's probably been sent away every summer since he could walk."

"Dude, what is your problem?" I'd been listening to Charles babble ever since we harnessed up with our partners and walked to the wall.

"I don't have a problem, not compared to the loser on the wall." Charles ran his free hand through his short hair. "Judging by the goods in his backpack he's up to his father's old tricks."

"Maybe you should mind your own business," I said, stepping away from him.

Charles shrugged. "Common knowledge is everyone's business."

"Uh . . . Shelby?" shouted Ariel.

I glanced up and realized she'd actually gone up a few feet. Her face was pale and she looked like she was about to cry. I released the rope a little through my guide hand. "Good job!" I yelled. "Climb on!" It felt better to focus on something other than Charles and his gossip.

She made a grunting noise and heaved herself to the next holds. She gazed down at me, and I could see the fatigue and fear in her face. She still had about thirty feet to go.

Charles shrugged. "I could tell you things about your new friend Austin that would make you freak. Ask him about Jillian Montrose."

"What? What the heck are you talking about?"

"Apparently, you don't read magazines," Charles said with a shrug. "Jillian, Austin's last little crush, had a total freak-out at his dad's estate. Claimed someone tried to attack her. Afterward, the Bridgeses sealed up that estate tighter than Willy Wonka's factory. No press have been allowed in for years. Not even *Rolling Stone*. There are all kinds of rumors about Austin's family being completely psycho."

"People always spread rumors about celebrities. That's what sells magazines, right?"

"Jillian never told the whole story, but from what I heard she was never the same. Maybe Old Man Bridges bought her off, or maybe she was terrified that Austin would come after her and finish the job. Anyway, I'd hate to think of you being next."

I gritted my teeth, wanting Charles to shut up. "Just because some girl spread some rumors doesn't mean the story's true."

"I'm just sayin', creepy is as creepy does. The Bridgeses aren't your average rock star family and Austin is the oddest one of them all. Who knows what really happened to that girl or what he's capable of."

"Why don't you leave him alone? Oh, wait, I forgot—your dad earns his living by making stuff up. It would be too much to ask to let people have their privacy, right?"

"Privacy is overrated," he said. "In fact, maybe you want to tell me what happened out in the woods before we showed up? There's probably a good story there."

"The only thing I'm gonna tell you is to shut up."

He laughed, which made me want to smack him, but then I heard a yelp. Ariel lost her foothold. The rope jerked in my hands and tightened in the belay device hooked to my harness.

"Help!" She swung her feet trying to steady herself, and then scrabbled her toes against the rock, trying to find another foothold.

"This is priceless," Charles said, snickering.

"Hold on!" I said, yanking the rope through my brake hand

to try to steady her so she could get to the next foothold. "Okay. Climb on!"

"I c-can't!" On the verge of crying, Ariel swung in her harness.

Everyone had stopped climbing to watch the spectacle of Ariel losing it. My stomach clenched with guilt. I hadn't focused on helping her make the climb. I'd let myself be drawn in by stupid Charles.

Even though it wasn't that far down, and she had a rope holding her, Ariel was clearly terrified. "Let me down," she said. "Ohmigod, let me down!"

"Go ahead and start lowering her," Cynthia Crumb said, a frown souring her face.

"Hurry!" called out Ariel.

Before I could even let out slack to start lowering Ariel, Austin swung across from his position on the rock and reached out. "I've got you," he said, putting a hand on her arm. "Relax. I won't let you drop." He was holding on to the rock wall with his left hand as he used his legs and hips to scooch closer to Ariel. One more step and he was right next to her, guiding her left hand to the nearest grip. "Now reach out a little to the right with your foot. There you go."

Ariel's feet found a place on the wall, and she let out a huge sigh.

I did, too.

Cynthia Crumb made a huffy noise behind me, like she couldn't believe Austin had actually done something good.

Meanwhile, Charles shook his head and readjusted Austin's rope in the belay device.

"Right, then. One step up," Austin directed.

Ariel gave him a scared look but then did as he said. He kept coaching her, and a few minutes later, she had climbed her way to the top, where Mr. Winters waited.

The old guy pulled her onto the platform and patted her on the back. "Good job, camper."

Ariel, still pale, nodded robotically.

Austin crested the wall and rushed over to Ariel. He wrapped her up in a hug. "That was brilliant," he said.

Something in me softened, seeing him holding her. I hadn't figured him for a hugger. He seemed distant and British and like someone who'd be more used to offering handshakes, but there he was, still with his arms wrapped around my new friend after saving her on the wall.

"Isn't that adorable?" Charles made a gagging sound. "A billionaire's daughter and a rock star's son. It's a little cliché, but—"

"Dude, shut up." I lowered the brim of my baseball cap and mentally tried to block him out. Above on the platform, Austin finally released Ariel, who was grinning. She waved down at me, and I waved back.

Austin gave me a little nod but didn't smile. Which was fine, because I was a bit confused at the moment. The drugs. The pain. Rumors spread by a freaked-out girl? And now this rescue mission on the wall? There was more to Austin Bridges than met the eye.

SEVEN

That night, sparks from Camp Crescent's bonfire flew up toward the dark sky like shooting stars in reverse. Conversations buzzed around the circle of log benches as the cliques of the camp formed. A cluster of Goth kids, minus black eyeliner, sat gloomily inspecting each other's empty piercing holes. A few of the chubbier campers debated the best s'more-making techniques. Some of the wilder boys were arm wrestling, their elbows anchored across the bench as they struggled.

All around the circle, the smell of burning sugar rose up from the marshmallows toasting in the fire. Ariel pulled at a sticky golden puff on the end of her stick, roasting the outside of the marshmallow, pulling it off and eating it, then roasting the new outsides. Marshmallows are okay, but I was seriously jonesing for some good old-fashioned gummy worms, which I was pretty sure Cynthia Crumb had devoured along with my romance novel.

I glanced over at Austin, sitting three logs away. His eyes reflected the gold colors of the bonfire, and the light of the flames flickered against his strong facc. Hc was staring at me. I felt weird—not bad, not good, just weird. I squirmed on the log, trying to get comfortable.

"Why is Austin staring? Do I have a zit or something?" asked Ariel, retreating beneath her bangs.

"No, no. It's not you. It's me."

"It's never me," said Ariel with a sigh. She stuffed her hands into the kangaroo pocket of her navy hoodie. "Well, unless you count that guy I met at archery today. Price. Price Fenton. He's from Georgia. I think he's a little odd."

"All the guys here are a little odd," I said.

"Oh, great," said Ariel as her marshmallow went up in flames. "Could you . . . oh, forget it." She suddenly threw her roasting stick down and scooched closer to me on the log bench.

"What's the deal?"

Ariel nodded across the campfire to where Charles was cruising for a seat. "He's so not sitting here."

"He's just another name-dropper," I said. "Don't give it another thought. My school's crawling with kids like him."

"I keep forgetting you're new, Shelby. It's way worse here," Ariel said. "People can be really cruel. Use stuff you say in group against you. Things like that."

We watched Charles take a seat on a log bench near the Goth kids.

"There. Safe." I picked up Ariel's roasting stick and handed it to her.

"Is this seat taken?" a short guy with a Southern accent asked Ariel.

Even in the firelight, I could see her cheeks pink up.

"Uh, no. Go ahead, Price," she said, giving me a look.

He plunked down and the two of them started talking. It was seriously cute. I could tell Ariel liked him because the blush in her cheeks never went away. She was totally absorbed in some story about Price's cat. I felt like a third wheel.

And then I saw Cynthia walk up with her guitar case. Great. What I really wanted, more than anything, was some peace and quiet. Back home, I spent a lot of time alone. On most weeknights, Priscilla would be off working out or shopping with her friends, and Dad had a lot of late meetings. That meant I had the whole house to myself. A quiet house, a good book, and a bag of gummy worms were sometimes all the comfort I needed. I wasn't used to the noise of living with other people or the incessant rounds of crappy camp tunes.

I knew it wasn't playing by the rules, but I felt like I had to be alone for a little while. I turned to Ariel. "Hey, if anyone asks, I went off to the bathroom. Do you mind covering for me?"

Not only did Ariel not mind, she didn't even look away from Price.

"'Kay, then. I'll be back," I whispered. I waited until a bunch of kids got up to get more marshmallows, and then I slipped away.

I've never been afraid of the dark. Sometimes my most favorite thing to do is soak in my tub with all the lights out. No candles. No music. Just the *plink-plink* of water dripping from the faucet. So peaceful.

Standing in the trees felt that way. I could watch the bonfire, barely hear the awful tunes coming from over there, and just be alone in the darkness. At least for a little while. During the second chorus of "YMCA," which I'm pretty sure was not written to be played on the guitar, I felt a hand on my shoulder. I jumped half a foot and almost screamed.

Austin.

"Thanks a lot!" I said, swatting him on the arm for scaring me.

"It's a pleasure to see you as well," he said.

I zipped up my sweatshirt, suddenly aware of the chill in the evening air.

Austin smiled. "The dark feels good, doesn't it?"

"You're supposed to be over at the campfire."

"As are you," he said with a little shrug.

I turned away, resting my back against a tree trunk. I tried to send a message with my body language, something along the lines of "leave now," but my stupid mouth kept on talking.

"Thanks again for helping Ariel."

He smiled. "All she needed was encouragement."

"You were good up on that wall. How'd you get over to her so quickly?"

"I'm rather agile," he said with a hint of a smile. "Anyway," he said, "thank you for defending my honor, as it were, with Charles. I saw him harassing you. I assume it was about me."

"Yep." My brain flashed back to what Charles had said. I didn't want to believe some stupid rumors, but a part of me wondered what had really happened to Jillian Montrose. I wanted to ask Austin about it, but I didn't want him to think I was the kind of person who believed everything people said or what was printed in tabloid magazines.

"I sensed you were a loyal person, Shelby. I appreciate your helping keep my family out of the spotlight."

"Of course. I wouldn't tell that guy anything," I said.

"Thank you."

We stood there for a moment, neither of us saying anything. The smell of burning sugar permeated the air all around us.

At last, Austin said, "Shelby, you've been terribly sweet, and I realize this may sound a bit forward, but I need your help."

I groaned. Here it was. The real reason Austin had found me in the dark. And the thing that sucked was that I already wanted to help him and I didn't even know what it was he was asking for. I gave him a hard look. "What do you want from me?"

"My serum. I have to have it. I can't do it alone."

My mouth dropped open. "You want me to help you steal

your drugs back? That's great, really great."

"It's not like that." His eyes darkened. "It's of vital importance I get that medicine. I have to have it before . . . well, let's say I have to have it as soon as possible. The dose I took in the limo is wearing off. I can feel it. I'll be sick at first, but after it works out of my system, it'll be mayhem."

"You're asking me to help you steal. That's like a one-way ticket to this desert hell camp my stepmother picked out for me! I can't go there. I mean, this place is bad enough."

"I know it's a risk." He took a step closer.

Now we were almost chest to chest, and I felt my knees sort of sway. I could smell the clean soapy smell of a fresh shower on his skin and the lingering sugary smell of marshmallows— which on a guy has to be the most delicious smell ever. Was it wrong to want a drug-crazed hottie to kiss me?

"It's not in my nature to ask for help, Shelby. I'm used to relying on myself. It's bloody difficult to be asking you for anything. I'm in dire straits." He licked his bottom lip. "Please, would you—"

"Wait," I murmured, my gaze tracking his tongue. "I know this part. This is the part where the sprinklers come on," I said.

"Sorry? What was that?"

Oops. I shook off the memory. "Uh . . . nothing. Look, there are better people to count on. Seriously. I'm, like, the least trustworthy person in the freaking universe—just ask my dad."

Austin frowned. "Do you always believe what other people say about you?"

I frowned back at him. "Okay, well, even if you wanted to count on me, I can't help you steal something. I can't break the rules. Seriously."

"You never were a rule follower before now, were you?" He said, his eyes intense. "You're here in the dark. You ran after me into the woods. You risked yourself to help me. No one ever did that for me. You're probably the only person in this bloody place who cares if I live or die."

"Live or die?" I crossed my arms against my chest. "Okay, let's cut to the chase. What are you into that you'd risk everything to get it back?"

Austin's smile faded. "I told you. It's medicine. That's the simple truth."

"If it's medicine, the camp would know about it, Austin. You have to put that stuff on your health forms."

"Graham, the new road manager, filled it out! He doesn't know the first thing about my family."

I shook my head. "I don't get you. You want to count on me and yet won't tell me the truth? You can't have it both ways."

"If I tell you, I must have your word that you won't tell another living soul."

"Okay, now you're scaring me. You make it sound like freaking top secret or something."

Austin lips twitched, and his teeth did that bitey thing on his lower lip. "The truth is," he said, "unfortunately, I have a disease."

"You have a *disease*?" It was impossible not to wrinkle up my nose, which was pretty judgmental of me. "Which one?"

"I hesitate to tell you," he said.

"You expect me to go down in flames for you and you won't tell me the truth?"

Austin's eyes shimmered gold in the low light as he scanned my face. He looked worried, tense, and that freaked me out.

"Uh . . . well?" I said, my voice coming out all nervous.

Austin glanced away, toward the campfire, and then, turning back to me, said, "Shelby, I'm a lycanthrope. What you'd call a werewolf. It runs in my family."

I swear my ears started ringing. "Holy crap. I thought you said you were a *werewolf*. What is wrong with my ears?"

Austin wasn't smiling. "I didn't expect you'd believe me at first," he said.

"What?" I gaped at him. "Are you serious? Dude, you can't be a werewolf. They're made up, and they're, like, dorky. I mean, except for that movie where there was this one wolf guy who was in love with a vampire. He was pretty cute for being a—"

"Shelby," he said, his mouth right up next to my ear. "I'm serious." As he backed off, his eyes reflected the light in an eerie nonhuman way.

I suddenly felt a bit wobbly on my feet. "You . . . uh . . . actually expect me to believe that creatures like that exist? That you're one of them?"

"Careful, you're talking about my family."

I shook my head. "Why would you say that? What is wrong with you?" I took a step back from him. "Oh, I get it. Joke's on me, right? Yeah, pretty good one, Austin. How did I not see it before—fangs, fur, howling at the moon? That's so hilarious."

"Shelby, this is no joke."

"Well, then, if you really think you're a werewolf you are totally mental. Not to be mean, but I guess I know why you're at brat camp."

His eyes darkened. "I am telling the truth. I'm not insane, and I'm not lying. You have to trust me."

Yeah. There it was. *Trust me.*

That was what they always said—what the freshman class's homecoming prince had said last year when he needed help picking out his tux and we got caught making out in the dressing room. *Trust me?* Yeah, right. I couldn't afford to trust anyone. I couldn't even *earn* anyone's trust anymore.

"I have to go," I said, feeling like I'd been splashed with icy water.

Austin grabbed my arm. "Believe me, Shelby. Why would I lie about this?" he said, steel in his voice.

"You tell me." I shrugged out of his grasp and walked back to the bonfire feeling annoyed. The hottest boy at camp was a complete liar. And he didn't even respect me enough to come up with a good lie.

I plunked down next to Ariel and Price and mumbled my way through a chorus of "She'll Be Coming 'Round the Mountain."

Austin never came back to the bonfire. Maybe he was trying to get his so-called prescription or maybe he was off howling with his wolf pack. *Right. Okay, so . . . whatever, Austin.* I told myself I didn't care. I wasn't going to wonder.

I grabbed the roasting stick from Ariel, and after eating a few gross but sweet marshmallows, I almost forgot about Austin and his bogus declaration. Almost.

EIGHT

*T*he next morning the girls' group session focused on just saying no to sex. Dr. Wanda, the psychologist, made everyone even more embarrassed than the day before. I mean, a grown woman asking if we'd hooked up before and then taking notes on it?

I decided, as did most of the smarter girls, to play totally innocent. I mean, not even my friends knew everything I'd done with boys. I told them the basic stuff, but there were some things I kept to myself. Some things I regretted a little. And Dr. Wanda thought I'd spill all my secrets in front of strangers? That kind of torture made weed pulling seem enticing.

As I worked in the flower beds around the dining hall later that morning, I watched for Austin to show up, but he never did. Meanwhile, Charles sweated away, hauling rocks and shoving them into place. A couple of times he shouted over to me, but I ignored him.

Later that afternoon, Ariel and I were on our way to the sand volleyball court. Cynthia had told the whole cabin to meet there for a bonding game, but so far we were the only ones headed that way. With all the weeding, I was missing out on camp sports. A friendly volleyball game would get my mind off stuff for a while.

"We're going to pass by the infirmary," Ariel said. "You know, if you decide you want to check on Austin."

"What?" I tugged down the edges of my University of Wisconsin T-shirt. It was the pink one that always rode up on my belly, but I loved it so much I couldn't bear to give it away.

"Well, Austin wasn't at lunch, so I asked Price and he said Austin got sick this morning. Probably allergies or a stomach-ache or something."

"Oh." Was he really sick? I remembered he'd told me last night that he'd be feeling sick off his medicine at first. Well, apparently, he'd made that part of the lie come true. Still, if he was telling people he was a freaking werewolf, he was either a pathological liar or completely mental. I doubted the nurse had a cure for that.

"So, do you want to go in?" Ariel asked. "I mean, I know you like him—I saw you talking to him in the woods last night."

I paused on the trail. For half a second I considered telling Ariel about Austin's crazy lie, but I remembered promising not to tell anyone. And I always kept my word, even to people who made stuff up. "He's got major issues," I said.

"Oh, and you don't?" Ariel gave me a questioning look as we

approached the infirmary. "He's probably in there. Maybe you should take a look. You know you want to . . ."

"I'm so not going in there," I said. "What would I say?"

Ariel rolled her eyes. "Oh, forget it. Stay here." She flung open the infirmary door and went in.

I wasn't going to leave Ariel, so I sat down on the wooden bench out front. After only about a minute, Ariel came out holding an ice pack on her forehead.

"Oh, crap! What happened?"

"Nothing," she whispered. "Start walking." When we got farther away from the infirmary, she lowered the ice pack. "I told the nurse I bumped my head on a bunk bed."

I gave her a doubtful look. "Um . . . you're totally short."

"Yeah, and apparently the nurse is totally dumb."

I smiled at her triumphant grin. "So . . . was he in there?"

Ariel let out a huge sigh as we sat down on the grass beside the volleyball court. "Uh, I don't know how to tell you this, but he was going through the nurse's purse."

Oh, great. Austin Bridges III was a kleptomaniac, too? I forced myself to forget all the other things I thought about him and focus on the facts.

"What was he looking for?" I said.

"I didn't get a chance to ask him."

"Well, how did he look?"

She shrugged and then gestured around at the volleyball court, which was starting to fill up. Humming, Cynthia Crumb marched past us with a net bag full of balls.

"He looked bad?" I whispered.

"He looked, um . . . scruffy. Like he needed a shave and a shower."

"Well, he's not exactly the type that'd follow a metrosexual skin regime," I said.

"Moisturizer is for everyone, every day," said Ariel with a bored smile. "At least that's DeVoisier Inc.'s motto."

"So what's really wrong with him?"

"Stomachaches are easy to fake at camp. The nurses always believe you because the food is mostly slop."

"Well, everyone knows his drugs are locked up with the contraband in Mr. Winters's office," I said, feeling a little Nancy Drew at the moment. "So what was in the nurse's purse that he wanted? A cell phone?"

Ariel raised her perfectly shaped eyebrows. "His dad's on safari. The manager hates him. Who else would he call?"

Ariel was right. I thought about Austin's distant family, about how he really had no one reliable to fall back on. Neither of us did, in a way. Did that mean it was okay to steal stuff, to tell crazy lies, to say things like "trust me" to someone who might almost be your friend? No way. You didn't treat your friends like that. And if that was the kind of person he was, then I needed to stay away from him.

But somehow I didn't want to.

What is it with square dancing? Why do old people think that it's even remotely fun? All that awkward hand-holding and twirling just made me dizzy and desperate for hand sanitizer.

Pretending I was tired, I sat out a dance, scanning the crowd that filled the barnlike gym that night. No Austin. He was a master at disappearing from things. I'd seen him briefly at dinner, but he hadn't looked my way once. Maybe he was angry at me about last night, for calling him a liar. But where was he now?

As Cynthia, the square-dance caller, droned on, I slouched on the bench, watching the dancers and being bored out of my mind. Ariel seemed to be having fun with Price. As they do-si-doed, he shoved his free hand through his dark bangs, combing them out of his eyes. Unfortunately, doing that revealed a bright crop of acne on his forehead. Still, he seemed nice, and he was totally into Ariel.

Actually, he was *on* her. Standing on her foot, I mean.

"My toe, my toe!" she yelped, hopping around.

A crowd gathered around Ariel. Poor Price went as red as ketchup.

I rushed over to where Ariel was now writhing on the ground. "Are you all right?"

She stopped writhing. "Duh. This is your chance to quit moping around and go find Austin," she whispered. "I think I broke my toes!" she whined to the crowd.

"You'll be all right," I said, helping her to a bench.

"Uh-oh," said Sven, rolling down Ariel's sock. "Lots of redness."

"We need the nurse," I said.

"It's her night off," Mr. Winters said in his booming voice. "We can do first aid. Don't worry, kids, I've got my kit right here."

"She needs ice," I said.

Mr. Winters smiled at me, and it was such a genuine smile, I kinda felt bad. But this show was all for a good cause. I had to keep going. "She's my friend, the least I can do is get her ice."

Mr. Winters nodded. "Very kind of you, Shelby. I'll trust you to go to the kitchen. Sweet Mrs. Neighbors, the cook, is probably about to close up for the night, so you'd better run. Just tell her I sent you."

"This is just great," Ariel said. "I'm the only camper in history to get hurt square dancing," she said, with an annoyed look. "How geeky is that?"

"Time for a sing-along," Cynthia Crumb called out as I left the gym. That was perfect. She'd be too wrapped up in the song to hunt me down for a little while. And by the time she did, hopefully I'd know what was up with Austin.

I wasn't sure exactly why I felt drawn to him. Maybe it was some sort of protective thing, or maybe it was just that out of everyone at camp he was one of the two people I actually felt a connection with. And seriously, though telling someone you're a werewolf is an obvious cry for help, he was entertaining and not bad to look at.

I decided to go find him along with the ice. At least that would get me away from the mindlessness of the square dancing, away from the kids who treated me like I was only cool because my dad was rich, and away from the adults who were trying to get me to open up.

As I headed out into the darkness, I told myself this was different from all the other times, that he was different from all the other boys. I just had no clue how right I was.

The path stretched out before me, gravel tinted pinkish by the fluorescent lights of the buildings ahead. A sliver of moonlight filtered through the clouds, crowning the evergreens along the path with silvery halos. Everything was quiet except for the hum of the electricity powering the lights and the buzz of insects.

I didn't have much time, so I ran to the infirmary first. I didn't see anyone, and the building was locked and deserted. So was the office. I doubled back and headed toward the cabins, but when I reached Sapsucker, no Austin.

Time was ticking by, and I still needed the ice. I booked up to the dining hall, its darkened windows looking like the hollow eyes of a sad face. The doors were locked. I knocked, but nothing happened. I could see a faint light radiating from the back of the hall, so I figured maybe the cook was in the kitchen cleaning. The pans from the chili dinner were probably pretty awful, especially the ones from the burned-tasting cornbread. I was so glad I'd been on weed duty and not stuck with dishes.

I rounded the back of the building, where there was a sort of alley. Sheltered by a stand of leafy trees, Dumpsters lined the far end of the collection of deep potholes and small patches of grass I'd be stretching to call a road.

One weak floodlight spilled a yellowish glow down onto the entrance of the road where I stood, but beyond that, it was all dark except for a square of light cutting into the gloom. Wait. The square was probably the window in the kitchen door. If the lights were on, the cook was still there. Ice, coming right up.

But first I had to charge down the dark alley, the exact opposite of everything anyone ever teaches you about personal safety. A light breeze stirred the leaves on the trees at the end of the alley, making a rustling sound that skeeved me out a little, but I walked forward, focusing on the light ahead, until I reached the door.

I was going to knock, but when I pulled at the handle, it gave way easily. It'd been propped open. Quietly, I stepped into the kitchen. The yeasty-sweet aroma of tomorrow's breakfast bread hung in the air. Mmm. The smell reminded me of my mom's homemade cinnamon rolls.

"Hello?" I called out. I peeked around the corner of the giant mixer toward the bank of sinks, but I didn't see the cook. Maybe she was off fixing her hairnet. "Um, I'm just here to get some—"

Slurrrggrrrfff!

A bizarre animal noise made me spin back toward the open kitchen door. I ran over and peered out into the alley. What the heck had made that sound? I took a few steps away from the door but noticed the floor seemed slippery all of a sudden.

I looked down.

Holy crap. Blood. A spattery blood trail I hadn't noticed when I'd come in, distracted by the cinnamon yumminess. At least I thought it was blood. It sure didn't look like ketchup.

The blood trail led to the kitchen, where I'd been before. What if it was the cook? Had something happened to that nice old lady? She could be hurt and I knew first aid. At the very least I'd assess the situation and then run and get Mr. Winters. I let out the breath I'd been holding and walked the edges of the blood-drop trail until it stopped at a giant silver door.

The walk-in refrigerator.

Uh-oh. I so didn't even want to know, but I had to check it out. I mean, it was ridiculous the stories my brain was spinning! It was probably nothing but a mess the cook somehow forgot to clean up.

I threw open the door and stepped inside. The cool air hit me like a snowball in the face. Hugging my bare arms around my chest, I looked around. Thankfully, I didn't see any hanging corpses stuck between slabs of beef.

In fact, there wasn't any hanging meat at all. Plastic bins, produce boxes, and industrial-size tubs of imitation nacho cheese sauce and "krab" salad filled the metal shelves that lined the walls. On the bottom shelf near some ugly-looking carrots, I found a white tub of meat chunks. Not New York steaks or anything but maybe pot roast, like the housekeeper had made for Dad's birthday this year.

Those meat chunks were bloody, all right, and there was a little pool of red in front of the tub, like someone had pulled a few pieces out of it. I sighed, relieved that at least I wasn't going to find the cook hacked up or anything. That's when I realized that the blood trail didn't lead in. It led out. Out to where the noise came from. Gross! Had someone killed the cook and dragged her outside?

I darted out of the walk-in refrigerator and sneaked toward the door, careful not to step in the blood again. As I passed the counter, I noticed the trays of cinnamon rolls rising near the ovens. That made me feel better. So the cook would be back soon, from wherever she'd gone. Listening more carefully now to the sounds coming from the main dining room, I could make out the laugh track of a television sitcom. She was probably vegging in her office while she waited to bake the rolls for the morning. Thank goodness she was all right. But what was up with the blood?

Slurrrggrrrfff! I heard the weird noise again, so I slipped out the back door and slid up against the building wall, listening. And then I heard a worse noise than the creepy sounds—the click of the kitchen door shutting. The door that had been propped open and was *now locked tight* when I jiggled the handle.

Slurrrggrrrfff! The sound came from near the Dumpster. It was like a wild animal eating something. Yikes.

I eased down the alleyway, still hugging the wall so whatever it was wouldn't see me going by. I would just sneak away

103

and it wouldn't even notice. Swallowing to clear my screaming muscles, I focused on staying calm, staying alert, staying invisible.

Slurrggrrrrrrr! The noise changed, going from a slurpy sound to a warning.

The hair on the back of my neck stood up. My throat felt all cloggy. Would I be able to scream for help or not? My heartbeat must have been about a thousand beats per minute because I suddenly felt like I was going to faint or something.

Luckily, my subconscious is a total hardass. *Wait,* it said, *remember what your dad told you about the woods—animals are usually more scared of you than you are of them. Suck it up and be brave.* I jumped out from the wall and said, "Hold it right there! Drop the pot roast!"

Okay, so in retrospect it wasn't the coolest thing to say. But the sound stopped. And a figure rose up behind the Dumpster. Everything was so dark at that end of the alley, I couldn't see for sure what it was.

I took a step closer. "Shoo! Uh . . . whatever you are!" I called out.

Now I could see it was a person—a guy. The dude had his hands on the Dumpster's lid now, like he was bracing himself. Totally creeped out, I started backing away.

"Stop," he called out. Just then the clouds parted, sending down a pool of moonlight over top of us. And I found myself face-to-face with the meat thief.

Austin.

In the moonlight, blood shimmered dark around his lips. His chin, also stained, looked scruffier than it had earlier, like he needed a shave.

"Shelby." He smiled, showing teeth whiter than I'd ever seen, way beyond the Zoom! teeth whitening Dad had let me get. And sharp, too, with pointy ends reflecting the pale light.

But they weren't the only things gleaming. His skin, his neck, his shoulders, his bare chest. Wait. *Bare chest?* He was topless in an alley, snarfing down raw meat?

"What, um, are you doing?" I asked, forcing myself to say something, anything. The hair on the back of my neck was still at attention, with some kind of follicle-deep sense of danger. I wrapped my arms around my waist, feeling an odd coldness.

He stepped out from around the Dumpster, and I instinctively moved back while trying not to stare at Austin's toned chest muscles and abs. "Don't be frightened," he said, his voice taking on a soothing tone. "It's only me."

Probably thinking I was gawking at the blood on his face, he swiped at his chin with his bare arm. Then he pulled on a black T-shirt he'd grabbed from behind the Dumpster. Casually, he said, "You've no reason to be frightened."

"Um . . . this is a little creepy."

He took another step forward, maybe expecting me to back up again, but I tried to be brave. My hands shook anyway, and my head filled with Charles's story about the girl who was attacked. Holy crap.

"So, I'm just going to mosey back to the square dance," I said, while in my head I flipped through the self-defense techniques my gym teacher had taught me that spring. My basic plan was to give him a swift kick in the groin and then run like hell.

Austin held up a hand, which, I noticed with a shiver, was dark with blood. "Please don't tell anyone," he said. "Graham will send me somewhere else, and the problem will only worsen. I need the serum in Mr. Winters's office."

I laughed nervously. "Right, the serum."

"I told you." He'd moved closer and was looking at me intently. His eyes flashed bluish silver, inhuman as they reflected the moonlight peeking through the clouds. "I'm Lycan."

Crap. I took a few steps backward. "No way. You—you are, aren't you?"

Austin Bridges III really is a werewolf! He wasn't a druggie. He wasn't mental. And he wasn't a liar. The one boy in camp I cared about had different problems altogether.

"Don't worry. The full moon's not for three days. I won't change against my will until then. You're safe," Austin said with a small laugh.

"Uh-huh." I tried to smile. "So, I'll just be going now."

"I know it's quite a lot to take in."

I glanced up the alleyway, mentally counting the steps to the clearing. "Look, I'd love to stay and be all Dr. Phil and everything, but I've got to get some ice for Ariel's fake broken toe before they send a search party after me. You might want to go in and clean up the blood trail you left in the kitchen."

He looked embarrassed. "I must have forgotten my manners being so famished."

"You better do it before the cook thinks there's been a murder. Oh, but the door's locked now."

"I'll boost myself through the window again," he said, shrugging. "It'll be quicker if you wait here and I fetch the ice for you."

Yeah, right! I was supposed to wait in a dark alley for him? "Umm . . ."

"You can't go back without it."

"No," I said begrudgingly. "I need the ice. But I'll meet you around front . . . in the light."

He shook his head at me, and then disappeared around the corner into the shadows.

Minutes later, I held the bag of ice for Ariel on my head, trying to dull the ache. I mean, I was glad that Austin wasn't a junkie, but how could this be real?

"Not what you expected, am I?" Austin said as we walked back to the square dance.

"Yeah. Not exactly."

We walked along in silence for a moment.

"So, what was with the pot roast? You, um, eat bloody stuff?" I said, trying to make conversation. I had no clue what I was supposed to say to a werewolf.

He nodded. "Off my serum, I crave it. Pure protein. The fresher the better. The cooked variety merely lays about in

107

my stomach—it doesn't satisfy the wolf's hunger."

"*The wolf* . . . you talk like he's a separate creature, but he's you. Right?"

Austin's eyes took on a serious look. "Yes and no. He's part of me. But that doesn't mean he controls me."

I gulped air past the lump in my throat. "So, uh, what does that mean, exactly?"

"We're two individuals sharing the same soul. We're together yet separate. Just like me, the wolf has his own instincts, desires, and thoughts."

"I don't get it. I mean, a wolf is a wolf, right? How can he think and stuff?"

"Werewolves aren't like regular wolves, Shelby. We don't always live or travel in packs like they do. We don't share the same social hierarchy. We aren't slaves to hunger like ordinary wolves. We are evolved beings. And when we change, we carry our human personalities with us. Even so, I've taken medication since I was twelve to suppress the wolf. It's easier for me to live that way."

"So, um, what about the wolf's feeding habits? I mean, should I be worried?" I said, my voice unnaturally high and squeaky.

He stopped, catching me by one arm. "Now that hurts my feelings. The notion that I would bite a friend."

"So maybe you wouldn't, but would the wolf?"

"No." He released my arm and we kept walking.

"So, did you change tonight? There's no full moon."

"The serum's out of my body. I felt ill this morning, but now

I can complete the transformation if I want to. It's easier for me to, ah . . . feed in my wolf body. It's far less revolting. When the full moon comes, I won't have a choice—I'll just change."

I nodded, totally getting why Austin would want the serum so badly. I had so many questions, but I was still freaked out. It was hard to wrap my brain around the whole idea.

"So, are you going to tell him or am I?" I asked when the campfire came into sight.

"Sorry. What?" Austin paused on the edge of the field.

"Are you going to tell Mr. Winters the truth? I mean, so you can get your serum?"

Austin's eyes got huge. "Are you daft? Neither one of us is. We can't tell him my secret," he said, his voice almost a growl. "The world catches wind of my family and we're dead."

"Oh." I pressed the ice bag to my head again. "So what are you going to do?"

"That's a question I've been trying to answer all week long," Austin said.

"Right." I lowered the ice bag and squinted at Austin in the dim light surrounding the volleyball court. He was telling me all this as if it were somehow my problem, too. Didn't the guy know I had my own issues at the moment?

"Why did you have to tell me?" I said, hoping it didn't sound too whiny. "I mean, I don't know what I'm supposed to do with this."

Austin's jaw set firmly. "You asked. I told."

My eyes widened. He just thought he could lay something

like that on me and life would be sunshine and rainbows? "Well, I didn't think the truth was going to be all supernatural," I said.

He looked at me, his eyes cold and silvery again, and said, "You asked for the truth. I thought perhaps that meant you cared." Then, without a backward glance, he disappeared into the night.

NINE

As if the square dancing the night before had been a bad dream, the giant barn-gym was transformed the next day and outfitted with a black wooden stage and rows and rows of folding chairs. Campers clustered in various parts of the room, trying to plan their talent show entries.

I stuck with Ariel while people chose groups, and it wasn't long before Price had worked his way over to us. Across the gym, Austin was sitting in a folding chair talking to two blond girls. I hadn't seen him interacting with any other girls at camp, and for some reason, seeing him do it made me feel a little weird. Not possessive, just weird. Like I should warn those girls that at any moment he might bust out some massive fangs.

My brain was still sorting through the events of last night, trying to see how it could have been real. I mean, if it were true, if creatures like werewolves lived among us, what other made-up things existed in the world? Seriously, any second now I expected Ariel to announce she was a vampire.

At that very moment, Austin looked my way. I gave him a half smile and then focused on the discussion my little group had under way. I didn't know what else to do.

"*Romeo and Juliet*?" offered Price.

Ariel smiled shyly. "Um, yeah . . . that's an idea."

"Maybe we could write a skit about the counselors? I know it's lame, but it'd be easy," I said.

Price and Ariel shared a look.

"What?"

"Everyone and his cousin's gonna do that," said Price. He frowned at the scratch paper in his hands. "That's why I'm thinking about some kind of real theater stuff."

Ariel nudged me and said, "He starred in his school's *My Fair Lady* last fall."

"Oh, cool. Well, whatever you think of, how about I paint the scenery or something?"

"I'd have a go at painting sets," Austin said, walking up to us.

Price beamed. "Great. Now we just have to find a copy of a play."

"Or Ariel could write one," I suggested.

Ariel's face went deep pink. "Uh . . . let's walk over to the camp library and see what's there," she said.

"Let's all go," I said, getting up from the chair.

Ariel put her hand on my shoulder. "You and Austin stay here and talk about set design stuff," she said with a wink. "I'm thinking some kind of fairy tale."

"That could work," Price said, nodding. "Let's go, Ariel."

"Shelby," Ariel whispered, leaning over to me. "I'm trying to help you out here. You can thank me later." With that, she and Price went off, chattering about their ideas.

Austin had taken a seat in an empty chair next to me. He glanced at me expectantly as I sank back down into my seat. "Frightened to be alone with me now?" he said.

"No. It's not that," I said. "I mean, it is kinda that, but kinda not."

"I expect it's difficult to grasp what you saw last night."

I blinked at him. "Uh . . . yeah."

Austin nodded. "You've taken it better than I thought."

"How was I supposed to take it? You told me you're not human."

"I didn't say that at all," Austin said, his eyes darkening. "We're humans with a genetic anomaly. We're far more human than most humans I know. Tell me, do I seem like an animal to you?"

I swallowed the response on my tongue—that any guy who would snarf down raw, bloody meat wasn't exactly normal. As far as him being human, he sure looked like a regular guy sitting next to me now, but in the dark last night he'd seemed like a ravenous wild animal. I wasn't sure what he—the wolf—was capable of.

He moved his chair closer to mine and said, "I'm not a mind reader, Shelby, but I can see you're frightened. You needn't be.

This is merely a genetic trait passed down through my family's bloodline. Though people have, over the years, infected others." He sat there, quietly watching me from behind his dark bangs.

I chewed at my lower lip. "So, your whole family is . . . ?" I leaned in closer to him and said, "I mean, you're, like, descended from a line of . . . people like you?"

Austin nodded. "My ancestors were the scourge of Eastern Europe in the twelfth century. Over the years, we've evolved. Our feeding habits are a lot more selective these days."

"Except for your father's," I said.

Austin colored slightly. "Yes. He enjoys the whole lifestyle. Howling at the moon, letting himself go wild out in the countryside. That's why we own several large estates. He loves working our private hunting grounds and going on safari. Of course, it's all nonhuman prey."

"What about your mom?" I asked, trying to sound casual.

The redness left Austin's cheeks and his body seemed to relax. "She wasn't born Lycan. She went through the change when she fell in love with my dad. Then Dad's band went worldwide and they could afford to hire the chemist who developed the serum. It inhibits the hormones that make me change and masks the parts of my DNA that are beyond human. Mum always wanted me to have a choice."

"She sounds cool."

"The best," he said.

"So there wasn't, like, any fortune of the werewolves or

114

anything? Your dad had to make himself rich?"

"We don't steal. You're thinking of vampires."

I did a double take. "So they *are* real, too? Holy crap."

He nodded. "Another genetic anomaly. Of course, they're the undead. We're very much alive."

"I still can't believe it," I said. "There're other people like you out there. For real?"

Austin seemed to brighten. "Yeah, world-renowned ones, too. Wrestling stars, heads of state, even a Miss Universe."

"She had to shave a lot, huh," I said with a little giggle.

Austin smiled but didn't laugh. "We're normal people with a horrible secret to bear. It's not like the movies."

"Yes, you're a very evolved community. You don't attack people. I feel tons better," I said, hoping Austin couldn't tell that I was still freaked.

"What do we have here?" Charles said. "Wasn't working out with the blond chicks, huh, Bridges?"

Austin glared. "We're having a private discussion. I emphasize the word *private*."

"Excellent. Don't let me stop you."

"What is your deal?" I said.

"Wow. She does like you! Unbelievable." Charles shook his head. "That's taking quite a risk. I guess you like to live on the edge, Shelby."

"What the devil are you talking about?" Austin stood up so that he was chest to chest with Charles. It looked like he was about to pop him a good one.

115

"I don't think you need me to repeat the story," Charles said casually.

"Searching for more lies?" I said.

"Searching for stories—not lies," Charles said. "This place is a gold mine of information."

"Stay away from me," Austin said, his voice almost a growl.

"Yeah. Not going to happen, Bridges. Not till I find out what's really going on with you. And I'll be keeping an eye on Shelby, too. I smell an exclusive." Grinning, Charles backed away and then walked off.

Austin slumped down in his chair. "That bloke is a problem," he said, closing his eyes. "Perhaps you see what my family's had to deal with. It's difficult enough keeping my father out of the press as it is. Not to mention our other problem."

"Yeah, if you don't get the serum and Charles sees you . . ." I murmured. If Austin changed in the middle of camp, not only could someone take a picture, but what if he was in his cabin at the time and couldn't get out? The kids might freak and attack him, or he them. I shuddered, thinking of how wolves ripped flesh from their prey.

"I'm sorry. It wasn't fair of me to involve you in all of this." Austin took one of my hands in his, and my first instinct was to pull my hand free.

But I didn't do it. I didn't want to let go of him. Austin seemed totally honest. I hoped he was telling the truth about the control he had over the wolf. I hoped he was the good person he appeared to be. And deep down, even though maybe it was one of my faults or whatever, I wanted to be able to trust him.

I let my hand relax in his grasp. It was hard not to notice how warm and dry his hand was as it wrapped around mine. I felt a little flutter start in my belly. He definitely was having an effect on me. One part fear, one part irresistible pull. And somehow it felt right.

The next day, while everyone hurried off to the boys' and girls' therapy groups, I walked directly to the camp director's office to scope out just what Austin was up against. There had to be some way to get to the serum.

A little nervous I'd be seen, I slipped inside the rustic office building and gently closed the door. No one was around. I walked to the office door and checked out the lock. It was pretty standard. I'd been hoping for a cheapie bathroom door variety you could pick with a butter knife.

The door to the building opened behind me, and I whirled around. In the same instant I noticed Mr. Winters and the security cam above the entryway—its red light blinking.

"Shelby? What brings you here?" Mr. Winters said.

"Oh. I was passing by on my way to group."

Mr. Winters smiled thinly. "You're late. Did you need to talk?"

"No, I, um . . ."

"Being late to group adds another day to your weeding chore," Mr. Winters said.

I pressed my lips together, holding back a curse. "Fine. I better go."

"Wait," Mr. Winters said, placing a hand on my shoulder.

"Yeah?"

We stood there looking at each other for a second before he said, "You came here to see me. What's on your mind?"

My friend is a werewolf who needs his medicine. "I, uh, was just coming to ask you if I had to garden again today, and now I do, I guess," I said, thinking on my feet.

"Shelby, you don't have to lie to cover your embarrassment," Mr. Winters said, shaking his head. He led me over to two chairs huddled in the corner near a dying ficus tree. "Look, I think I understand why you're here. Of all the young women at camp, you have a real chance at remaking yourself, if that's what you'd like to do. I hope you're here because you want to talk. I hope you're perceptive enough to realize that you are the only one who can change the direction of your life."

"I don't think it's going in such a bad direction," I said, feeling just a bit uncomfortable now. I prepared myself for the onslaught of professional advice that was sure to come. So much for an easy reconnaissance mission.

"Shelby, your father wrote on your application a little of your recent family history. I'm sure you've probably heard this, but losing a parent is one of the hardest things a child can experience."

I gritted my teeth. I *had* heard that before—from everyone who looked at me with the poor-Shelby expression and whispered about me as they walked away. It was cold comfort to have people pity you.

He continued, undeterred by my stony glare. "You're a strong, obviously brave young woman after surviving that kind of loss," he said. "No one can prepare a kid for that pain. It takes courage to go on after that."

I blinked. "As if I had a choice in the matter," I replied.

"Actually, you did." Mr. Winters gave me a sad smile. "And I have a feeling, knowing you even for a short time, that you were staying strong for your dad. You probably felt like you had to be strong for him."

I sucked in a deep breath, wishing the conversation was over. "Look, I just did what I had to do."

"I've known a kid or two in similar circumstances. You didn't break down. You didn't want your dad to see you sad because you thought he was already sad enough. But, when you're young, parents are there to support you, not the other way around."

"You're making a lot of assumptions," I said.

He smiled again. "Why don't you tell me how you see it?"

I shook my head, my eyes tight against the tears I could feel behind them. I wasn't going to do it. I wasn't going to cry. Not in front of some random counselor guy who thought he knew me after a few days of pulling weeds with him.

He patted me on the shoulder. "It's okay. I want you to know everything you're feeling, and everything you felt back when your mom died, is okay. It wasn't your fault. There was nothing you could do but love her, which obviously you did very well."

I wiped my moist eyes with the sleeve of my hoodie, but I didn't say anything. I didn't know where this old guy got off saying all this stuff when he wasn't there, he couldn't know how I'd felt, even if he was a good guesser.

"That's right—just go with the feeling," Mr. Winters said.

I sniffled. "Uh, I should go, girls' group and all. Fun, fun, fun."

"You don't like girls' group?"

"What's not to like?" I said with a laugh. "Another session of let's talk about becoming a woman? Who wouldn't love it?"

He didn't react to my sarcasm. "You find it boring?"

I rolled my eyes at him. "It's embarrassing and totally unnecessary. I'm sixteen. Technically, I'll be an adult soon. I don't need to hear all this becoming-a-woman crap. In a couple of years I'll be off at college far away from rules and stepmothers and people like you who think I'm some kind of head case."

"I don't think that, Shelby. Do you?"

Gah! I stared at him and said, "No, I don't think that. I'm perfectly fine."

"You sound pretty angry for someone who feels fine."

"Duh! I'm angry at people butting into my business and telling me what to do and who to be and what to feel."

He cocked his head at me, looking like some kind of hairless St. Bernard with that big head of his. "That makes sense, Shelby, but following your parents' rules builds trust between you and them. Consider it logically."

"Sure. Are we done?"

He nodded, so I walked to the door.

"Enjoy girls' group," he said. "I'll see you in the flower beds after."

"Yeah, great." Forcing myself not to slam the door, I left the building. I felt truly angry. It was easier to be at home where nobody talked about all this stuff than to be here where adults who barely knew me made a bunch of assumptions. I was totally fine—and other people had way worse problems than I did. Problems that were supernatural.

The rest of the day went by slower than ever, beginning with the weediest flower bed I'd done yet and ending with the most boring of all of Dr. Wanda's lectures instead of a campfire. It was all about the transformation ceremony we were supposed to have in a few days.

That night I was so tired I fell asleep almost as soon as I zipped up my sleeping bag. I dreamed about Orlando Bloom, who I'd once seen in real life, shopping at Beverly Center. In the dream, I was working on his movie set as a script supervisor, and he kept asking me for his lines. Then he asked me to come to his trailer and help him rehearse. I was about to follow him when . . . *bam*!

My eyes popped open and I sat up straight in my bunk in Spotted Owl. That was definitely not a forest noise. Maybe it was a shutter banging in the wind or a loose screen door. A line of goose bumps traveled up my arms.

I glanced around the dark cabin, barely lit by the moonlight peeking in through the far window. No one else was awake or even seemed to notice the sound I heard, though Cynthia snorted in her sleep and turned over on her cot near the door.

Go back to sleep, I told my busy brain. I settled back into my bunk and shut my eyes hard.

Eeeee! I heard the squeal of something, some animal.

That was it. I sat up again and reached down into my backpack to get a flashlight. What if it was Austin out there? A chill whispered over my skin, but a part of me really wanted to see him do it—change into a wolf.

I put a hoodie and yoga pants on over my cami and shorts and stuck my feet into a pair of flip-flops. But tiptoeing in flip-flops was hard, so I took the things off until I got by Cynthia's bed. Then I nudged open the door and eased out onto the porch.

The nearly full moon cast eerie shadows on the trail in front of me, and the gravel seemed unnaturally white in the glow. I stepped into my flip-flops and then down onto the—

Eeeee!

I froze, trying to figure out where it was coming from. Up the trail. Up the trail toward Sapsucker, it sounded like.

122

Flip-flopping as quietly as I could, I moved toward the sound, passing Squirrel, Mule Deer, and Muskrat cabins really stealthily. Well, at least until I tripped over a vine and went crashing into the gravel. Wincing, I brushed the pebbles off my pants and continued moving on in the moonlight.

The evening air shimmered around me, cool and moist, nothing like the dry summer air back in So Cal. I wondered what my friends were doing down in Cabo right then—definitely not worrying about brat camp werewolves.

The trees got thicker, casting more sinister shadows on the bright gravel, so I clicked on the flashlight. It didn't help much. And after a moment, I realized it probably would give me away, so I turned it off, relying on the moon. The same moonlight that would cause Austin to change against his will in two more days.

Eeeee! The squeal started up again. Or was it a new squeal? It had to belong to something small, but this time it was louder.

I ducked behind some trees, taking the roundabout way to Sapsucker cabin so I wouldn't be seen. Ahead of me, behind the cabin, there seemed to be a trail cut in the brush. One of those animal paths I'd seen back in the forbidden forest. All of a sudden, the bushes at the entrance to the path quivered. *Grrrrrr!*

The hair on the back of my neck stood up and my heart shook in my chest.

Eeeee! The squeal rose from inside the bushes, and then something worse than any noise I'd heard before—slurping.

The squeaking victim was being eaten. Oh, man. Forget it! I didn't want to see that carnage.

I backed up, one flip-step at a time, until I was in the grassy area away from the trail. Then I stepped on something solid yet mushy.

Horrified, I clicked on the flashlight and looked down. All around my feet were what looked like dead opossums. Or what was left of them. Little pink tails, fleshy paws, gray fur balls matted with blood. I started running. Flip-step, flip-step, flip-step. Then I thought I heard the sound of something behind me, following me at top speed.

I kicked off the stupid flip-flops and ran barefoot on the dirt sides of the trail. Running so hard I felt like my heart was going to explode, I flew down the trail. I was almost there. I was actually going to make it.

And then I tripped on that stupid vine. Again.

That's always the part in the horror movies when the cute girl gets slashed. She's clueless, then curious, then dead. I *so* didn't want to be that girl.

I rolled over and scrabbled backward on my hands and feet, watching for whatever was trying to run me down. I was going to meet the thing head-on, fully aware as I died on a gravel trail in the middle of Nowhere, Oregon.

After a few seconds of terror, nothing had killed me. No killer, no creature, no slasher seemed to be around so, heart still pounding, I stood up and dusted off my yoga pants. Something *had* been chasing me. I was pretty sure of that. But now I could only hear the chirp and whir of insects active in the night.

At least, until Austin stepped out of the bushes. "Here you are," he said, holding out my flip-flops.

I took the sandals from him and whacked him on the arm. "You scared me!"

"Shelby, what did you expect? You startled me while I was feeding!"

"Well, sorry. I didn't mean to. And, um . . . what was with the opossums?" I said, wincing.

Austin's cheeks flushed. "Ah, forgive me. Fresh meat and all that."

"Dude. Eww! We've got to get you the medicine," I said. "And the chasing me? Not cool."

"Again, sorry," he said. "It's an instinct thing. Running prey. Terribly sorry." He crossed his arms.

"An instinct thing?" I said with a shiver.

"The wolf's. Not mine, obviously."

"Oh." I stared at his Burning Bridges T-shirt; it was hanging unevenly from the waistband of his jeans like he'd gotten dressed in a hurry. Duh! Of course, a minute before, he'd been . . . um . . . naked? I jerked my head up to his face, my own cheeks feeling hot and scratchy. "So, you've been snacking. Did it help?"

He shrugged. "It was something, at least," he said with an unsure smile.

I slipped the flip-flops onto my feet. "So, I checked out

the door to the office."

"You did?" He looked the happiest I'd ever seen him. It kinda freaked me out. I took a step back. "Shelby, I—"

"Shh!" I said, pointing at the cabin door about twenty feet from us. I was nervous Cynthia would wake up and come looking for me.

"C'mon," he said. "This way."

We walked over to the abandoned campfire pit, figuring that way we would see anyone coming. As we took seats on a log bench, Austin reached into his front pocket.

"Ariel told me, you, um . . ."

"No way! Gummy worms?" I took the little bag from his outstretched hand. My heart started a skippy dance in my chest.

Austin shrugged. "Gummy *bears*, I'm afraid. The nurse thought I needed something to cheer me up."

"Yum!" I tore open the package and handed him a few. "You have no idea how much I missed gummies."

"Rather good," he said through a mouthful of candy.

"The best." I ate three, chomping the heads off and then popping the squishy bodies into my mouth. I could tell from the sweet fruity taste they were the red ones. *Yum*. I sighed as the sugar cleared my head. I tossed back the last of the gummies, relishing the silky texture. "So how are you going to get your serum? Your dad's manager can't help, right?"

"Definitely not. Winters and I called him on speaker phone and he said, 'I'm the best manager in the UK because I don't put up with any band's crap addiction issues. Why, before I came to work for your father, I saved a diabetic drummer from his self-destructive sugar cravings.'" I laughed at the thick cockney accent Austin poured on. "'Not to mention the pop star I saved from frittering away her royalties on her shoe-shopping binges,'" he said. "'A personal crusade, it was.'"

"Nice."

Austin nodded. "Unfortunately, Graham knows nothing about the family situation. Dad's only just hired him. The last guy, he didn't work out."

"Did your dad, um . . ."

Austin gave me a disappointed look. "He sacked him. He didn't eat him. My dad prefers wild meat. That's why he chose the hunt in Kenya for his holiday. We don't eat people, remember? Well, unless they're really, really naughty."

I gasped.

"Joking, only joking. Anyway, Dad's chemist is the only one outside the family who knows the truth."

"If you could only get in touch with the chemist dude, you'd be set."

"Exactly," Austin said, sounding defeated. "But every bloody phone in this place needs a code. And I've looked everywhere for a cell phone."

"Okay, that's what Ariel saw you doing, that day in the nurse's office. . . ."

He smiled grimly. "I wasn't after her lipstick. I need a phone."

"Or you could steal the serum from the office—which has a security camera."

He nodded. "Right. I'd be caught on tape. Forget Charles and his nonsense—the real paparazzi would be on my family like a plague of locusts. If anyone found out about our family's hairy little problem, my dad would be . . ."

"You don't want to lose another parent."

He looked at me cautiously. "You know about my mother?"

"Ariel told me."

"She died on a night hunt with my father in Scotland six years ago. Quite a scandal. Dad went through an inquest—but he was proven innocent. Of course, what the papers didn't say was Mum was shot as a wolf but died in her human form."

I recognized the pain in his voice. It was all too familiar. "Um, listen—"

"It's quite all right," he said, holding up a hand. "Sympathy gets to be old hat after a certain point."

"No, um . . ." I swallowed past the lump in my throat, the taste of candy gone. "My mom. She died three years ago."

Austin lowered his hand. "Oh. I didn't know."

"No one here knows," I said.

"I'm sorry."

I shrugged. "Like you say, sympathy gets old. I don't tell people anymore."

Neither one of us said anything for a while, but somehow it was okay. We were just together but alone on that bench. After a while, I felt Austin's hand reach for mine. His fingers were warm, and when they squeezed mine, it didn't even occur to me to pull my hand away.

"Now you know all my secrets," he said.

Actually, I didn't know all his secrets. I still couldn't bring myself to ask him about Jillian Montrose, but after being chased tonight, I wondered just how much control Austin had over the wolf.

"It's only fair that you tell me yours," he said.

I wrinkled my nose at him. "I don't have any secrets."

"Not true. There's something there, something sad in you that I sensed from the first time I saw you on that bus."

"Duh. I miss my mom." I gave him a weak smile.

"I miss mine as well, but beyond that." He squeezed my hand again, only this time, instead of the butterfly feeling in my stomach, I felt a warmth spread all through my body. Austin pulled me a little closer, until my head was almost resting against his shoulder, and said softly, "Your secrets are safe with me. I mean, unless you're planning to run off and scream 'Werewolf!' at this very moment."

There was a smile in his voice, but I didn't look up because I had the feeling the second my face was close to his I was going to do something really stupid like kiss him. What would it be like to kiss Austin? To kiss him under the half moonlight. Him, someone I should probably run from, but the one person who seemed to really get me.

"Come on, what's your secret? Tell me."

In an embarrassing gush of honesty I said, "I'm afraid I'm losing my dad, too." Then, what was totally worse, I actually started crying a little.

"It's okay," Austin said. He kissed the top of my head and let go of my hand so he could wrap an arm around me. "He's not going anywhere."

I brushed tears from my cheeks with my right shoulder, fully humiliated for him to see me like this. "I haven't seen much of my dad this past year," I said. "He's got this stupid new wife. I hate her. All he does is chase her around and take her advice, and it's like Mom never even existed. I can't even remember the last time the two of us did anything together. No, wait, we hung out with the principal when I got suspended."

"The headmaster of your school?"

"Yeah, there was this whole skirmish with the freaking debate team captain, but it was totally her fault."

Austin smiled. "You've got serious *joie de vivre*."

I felt a fluttering feeling in my stomach again. Was he actually complimenting me on my bad decision making? I smiled, but then I realized I'd totally forgotten about that whole don't-get-close-to-his-face rule I'd made up. My lips were only millimeters from his lips.

Wait . . . a few minutes ago he'd been killing little creatures. He'd been an animal with sharp teeth. An animal that had chased me down the path. My heartbeat quickened, but I forced myself to relax. This was Austin. He was just a guy sitting with me in the faint glow of the moon. Just a guy. My gaze traced the curve of his lips. He was only a boy . . . a boy I shouldn't be—

I moved back before my lips did something stupid. "Let me think of something. Okay? There's got to be a way we can keep you safe."

"Thank you." He cupped my cheek with his hand, and I saw a flicker of silver in his eyes. I fought down a shiver of fear mixed with something else. I really was scared of what he'd become when he changed. What if he was sugar-coating the truth and I was in trouble? Well, me and the whole camp full of kids.

He moved his hand away, like he'd sensed the fear stirring inside me. "I should go," he said. "Can you find your way back to the cabin all right?"

I nodded, and he strode off toward the path to the cabins without looking back. So much for near kisses and gummy bears. I bit my lower lip, a strange feeling growing inside me as he faded in the distance. How could I want to protect someone I was scared of at the same time?

I stood up from the log and moved toward the path, the beam of the flashlight the only thing keeping me from being alone in the dark.

"Out for a stroll?" A voice cut through the night a minute later as I made my way back to Spotted Owl.

I whirled around and saw Charles leaning against a tree on the side of the trail. My breath caught in my lungs. "I, um—"

"Moonlight is so peaceful," he said. Half in shadow, his face took on sharp angles, making him look less like a squinty-eyed Brad Pitt and more like a blond Joaquin Phoenix. "What are you doing out here?" he asked, moving into the light.

I shrugged, trying to look casual as I took a step back from him.

Charles crossed his arms against the chest of his T-shirt. He was dressed in all black like some kind of burglar from a bad movie, which was a far cry from his usual outfits of layered polo shirts and khaki shorts.

I consciously smoothed out the wrinkles in my brow. "What are *you* doing out here?"

He gave me a smug grin. "Not very good security at this place, is there? If the two of us can be out and no one notices."

"Hello? No security? There's a huge fence around this place."

He nodded. "Yeah. But you could smuggle all kinds of stuff in. I mean, look at your friend, he had quite the stash."

"What did he ever do to you?" I said.

"It's not what he did *to* me, it's what he could do *for* me."

I put my hands on my hips. "You better stay away from Austin."

Charles pressed his thin lips together. "This is the story. And let's face it—with his history, it can only get bigger."

"You're classy, you know that?"

He shrugged. "It's nothing personal. I just want out of this place. As soon as I get some hot copy and pictures, I'll be on the next plane. My dad can't resist a scandal—especially one involving the Bridgeses."

"You want to go home that bad?"

"Home? Uh, boring! I'm thinking Ibiza or Mykonos. There's a whole summer of parties ahead."

I rolled my eyes. "Look, you're not going to get anything on Austin. There's no scandal here. You better find another target. Or how about this—make some friends and try to have a good time at camp."

Charles shrugged and for a moment looked almost sad. "Do you have any idea how hard it is for me? I mean, the famous kids I know are always afraid I'm gonna tell my dad stuff, and the regular kids keep trying to be my friend to get themselves on TV. It's not easy."

"Everyone has it tough, Charles. That doesn't mean you should exploit people. I mean, you might even make a friend if you didn't try to use them."

He stood there looking at me for a moment. "Yeah, maybe," he said. "But that's not going to happen, so why try?" He gave me a finger wave and then walked off down the trail.

I made my way back to Spotted Owl, now more worried than ever about Austin. And knowing if Charles got his hands on the real story, it'd be all over.

TEN

The next morning I was finishing up another weedy flower bed when Mr. Winters appeared, casting a huge shadow over me. "How's it coming?" he asked after a moment.

"Pretty good."

"Good." He kept standing there, watching me work.

That annoyed me to no end. "Um, is this the part where you ask me about my mother again, and I go all weepy and then we hug it out and you consider the whole thing a raging success?" I said, dropping a shovelful of dandelion roots at his feet.

Kicking the stuff aside, he smiled down at me. "Actually, I was coming to tell you you've completed your work sessions."

"Oops," I said. I smiled in the hope that he'd let my snarky comment slide. "So, I'm all cured, then? I don't have to do any therapy stuff with you?" I asked.

"Working on yourself is an ongoing process. Dr. Wanda has

offered to give you individual appointments if you think you need them."

Ugh. I shivered on the inside. "No way. I mean, no, I don't think that'll be necessary, thanks anyway."

He nodded, slipping his hands into the front pockets of his khaki shorts, which just seemed to make his tummy stick out more. I expected him to leave, but he kept hanging.

"So, was there something else?" I asked. I scratched my cheeks against the shoulder of my yellow Juicy T-shirt—not the best weeding attire, but wash day wasn't until next Monday, and I was nearly out of clean Ts.

"I wondered if you thought over what we talked about," he said.

"I knew this was going to be about my mom dying again," I said, rolling my eyes.

He smiled and took a seat next to me on the ground. "You know, when something bad happens and you don't get a chance to get those feelings out, you delay the pain, but you don't get rid of it. It stays inside you, taking up space."

"I guess."

Mr. Winters shrugged. "I've heard you talk about being angry at your stepmother, but how about your father? What's going on there?"

"It's not good," I said quietly.

He nodded. "It hasn't been easy for either of you."

"Yeah. I guess." I brushed a clump of dirt off my leg. I didn't want to look Mr. Winters in the eye. I didn't want to think about how hard it'd been for my dad. That stuff about delaying pain—that's what he'd done in marrying Priscilla. I mean, how could he have mourned Mom and moved on so quickly? It still felt so fresh to me.

Mr. Winters nodded. "Okay, then we're done here. I've told Cynthia to expect you in about ten minutes over at the talent show rehearsals."

"I'm not performing," I said with a shrug. "I'm helping with scenery."

He gave me a small smile. "That's great. We all have different talents."

"So I'm supposed to just leave all this?" I gestured to my unfinished flower bed and the small pots of violets and pansies waiting to be planted.

"There's always someone who could use a morning gardening," Mr. Winters said, taking the tools I handed him. "And if you'd try to have some fun now that the work's over, Shelby, I'd appreciate it."

In the gym my favorite werewolf stood poised with a paintbrush. In front of him white clouds swirled over dark blue sky, and green thickets of vines twined up the sides of the canvas flats. Little birds perched on rose branches near a stone fountain gushing clear sparkling water. It was a forest paradise.

"Austin," I said as I approached, "this is amazing."

He turned, half smiling. "Ariel kept mentioning a forbidden

forest, so I painted it for her. Ah . . . you weren't here, so I
began. I hope you don't mind."

"Mind? Holy crap! This is the most beautiful scenery I've
ever seen."

"Oh. Well, thank you." A blush crept into Austin's cheeks,
which made me smile. "I do a bit of sketching." He set his
paintbrush down onto an aluminum pie tin he was using as a
palette.

"So, what are we doing?"

He wiped his hands on a cloth. "It seems Price and Ariel
decided on *Beauty and the Beast* this morning. Ariel will write;
Price will direct."

"*Beauty and the Beast?*" I blinked at him. "Um . . ."

"The fairy tale, not the Disney movie," Austin said. "Ariel
argued with Price about the corporate implications."

"Oh. And you're *okay* with *Beauty and the Beast?*"

"I'm just doing the scenery, Shelby. Nothing more."

"No, I mean . . ."

"I'm well aware of the story," Austin said, sitting down next to
me. Up close, I could see a little splotch of yellow paint, round as
a moon, on his cheek. I wanted to rub it off, but I didn't.

"Listen, I wanted to tell you something, but I didn't get a
chance at breakfast with everyone around," I said. "Last night
Charles was on the path when I walked back to my cabin. He
obviously was stalking you. He's trying to make you into some
kind of tabloid story."

Austin shook his head. "I'd already figured as much."

"No, I don't think you get it. He's a serious problem," I said. "What if he has a camera and gets pictures of you changing or whatever?"

"They confiscated all cameras," Austin said.

"He's sneaky. And *you* have stuff you're not supposed to have, like your matches. He could have a camera."

Austin smiled grimly. "If I don't get the serum in the next two days, I'm not going to be around for him to take snapshots."

I felt a little sinking feeling in my stomach. "You'd leave? You said there was no reason to worry, that you don't attack people."

"And I meant it." Austin's mouth pulled into a grim line. "I thought I could just hide out in the woods around the cabins at night, but it's too risky. Someone might see me. I can't put my family in jeopardy." He stared down at his hands, one finger scratching at some red paint speckles. "You're only the second person I've ever told my secret to," he said quietly.

"Who was the other one?"

He studied my face for a moment and then said, "Jillian Montrose."

I inhaled a deep breath. "The girl who spread the rumors."

He nodded. "We were schoolmates when I was twelve. My first crush, I guess you could say. I told her the truth and she laughed and told me being a werewolf was fine because she was a sorceress."

My eyes widened. "And was she?"

"No, no. She was playing along. We were the best of friends.

But then her family came to our estate for the weekend when my father was away touring Japan. No one realized I was on the edge of my first change."

"Nothing happened, right?"

"It was the weekend of a bloody full moon, Shelby."

My heart stilled. "Oh, no."

"It was a summer night, and Jillian and I were up late watching the telly. We went out to the garden to get some air. She was dipping her toes into the fountain while I was picking strawberries near the fence. But then the moonlight hit me. The next thing I knew I was transforming into my wolf body. It terrified me. I'm not certain what Jillian saw, but as I ran off into the woods to hide, I heard her screaming. In the morning I woke naked in an open field. When I made it home, my governess had the police searching for me, and Jillian's family was tearing down the drive in their Range Rover. They thought something awful had happened to her."

My skin prickled with goose bumps. "So she saw you change," I said. "And she freaked out."

"I don't know. It's all a blur. But I didn't attack her; I ran away—afraid of what I had become. The constable leaked the story of the incident to the London press, and the rest of the year was a nightmare. Jillian kept quiet—but she never spoke to me again. I probably mentally scarred her for life. I still feel horrible about the whole thing."

"Austin, I'm sorry that happened to you."

He looked embarrassed. "Forgive me. I don't mean to

burden you with more confessions." He paused, squeezing my hand. "But now you see that I can't take a chance with the press again, even if it means I leave someone I care for. And I do care for you. You must know that."

There was a tender look in his eyes now, and it only added to the mixture of attraction and fear I was feeling. I forced myself to breathe. He was waiting for me to say something, so I mumbled, "Yeah."

"I haven't experienced the lunar change in years—since that first time. I've heard it can be unpredictable. And now that I'm grown, I imagine it will be stronger than it was before." Austin looked out across the gym at the other groupings of kids working on their sets and costumes. "I hate this," he said finally. "I would rather be anything but this."

My heart smashed into a thousand little pieces for him. I felt the need to say something, anything, to make him feel better. But I didn't know what that might be. I could see why he hated the change, why he suppressed the wolf. There was reason for him, and maybe for all of us, to be scared. But at the same time, this boy was just Austin. An artistic, caring, intelligent guy who was anything but beastly.

"So, what can I do to help you? I mean, with the sets," I added, clearly needing to change the subject. I pushed the wolf out of my mind and focused on the cute boy in front of me.

Austin gestured toward the paints and brushes. "You could fill in the leaves on the rosebush," he said.

I nodded and stood up.

"Shelby, thank you for listening."

"That's what friends are for."

He smiled weakly and got up. "I haven't many of those. You're the first in a long, long time. As you can imagine, it's near impossible to trust anyone."

"Yeah, I can see."

He gave me a grateful look and then walked over and picked up his paint palette and brush. We worked without talking until we had finished the forest tableau. Of course, I only added a few highlights here and there to the beautiful scene Austin had crafted, but when we were done, I felt a sense of satisfaction. We'd created a perfect, idealized background for *Beauty and the Beast*. And I didn't want to think about what that symbolized any more than Austin did.

ELEVEN

"Take the raffia and simply twist it into bird wings like so," Dr. Wanda said, running a special arts and crafts session the next day after lunch.

The other counselors had some kind of meeting, so instead of cramming into the tiny art studio, all of us campers were in the dining hall, spread out among the lunch tables. Hardly anyone was paying attention to Dr. Wanda.

"Then, using another piece of twine, tie those wings to the body of the bird," she said, walking between the tables and then stopping at mine. "Austin, there's room over here. Why don't you join this group?"

My head jerked up. I hadn't seen him at breakfast, and I had been wondering what he was up to. My heart beat a little faster just seeing him in the entry of the dining hall. He wore a black T-shirt and jeans, his brown hair pushed back behind his ears. He saw me and smiled. I let out a breath I'd been holding. He looked so normal. Well, gorgeous and normal.

Dr. Wanda waved Austin over to our table. "Just start here. Price can show you what to do."

"Sure thing, Dr. Wanda." Wearing his usual grin, Price slid his project down the table to make room, so that Austin was directly across from me. "Here's some raffia," Price said, handing him some materials. "We're making big ol' birds."

"Thanks, mate. Hello, Shelby," he said.

"Hey," I said casually, but my voice sounded small and far away. My palms felt sweaty, so I wiped them on my shorts.

"Okay, what you do is . . ." Price began, rattling off the bird directions Austin had missed.

"Hey, Dr. Wanda! Mine looks like a spider," Jenna said a minute later, waving her hand to get Dr. Wanda's attention. "Have you had formal art training or did they teach you this in shrink school?"

Dr. Wanda smoothed her frizzy bangs and then pulled at the hem of her shirt, which barely covered her round middle. Obviously, the woman was trying to keep it together. If it were me, I'd probably have told Jenna where to stick it, but Dr. Wanda managed to smile. "All of us are making birds that express our individuality. Every bird has a chance to fly, eight legs or not."

Jenna grunted and went back to tying her deformed wings.

"We'll be having a fire circle ceremony on the full moon tomorrow night," Dr. Wanda continued. "Your bird represents the old you, and by burning it in the bonfire you'll be releasing your new spirit to fly."

"Burning them is supposed to help them fly?" Jenna said, rolling her eyes. "That is such crap. I hope this raffia isn't treated with toxic elements that'll form dangerous fumes when it's incinerated."

Dr. Wanda smiled, still ignoring Jenna. "The full moon is the perfect time for beginnings. Many ancient societies believed full moons possess magic."

Price grinned. "That's a big night in Savannah. Voodoo priestesses, cemeteries at midnight, all that."

"You actually believe in that drivel?" asked Austin with a nervous laugh.

"My momma says it's true, and I don't need to find out for myself," said Price. He gave the sleeves of his rugby shirt a little push up his forearms and went to work tying on big, goofy bird wings.

"I need to talk to you," Ariel whispered and led me over to the supply table. "I think Price really likes me," she said, pulling more blue raffia from a box. "Did you see him take my tray to the kitchen at breakfast? I didn't even ask him to do it!"

"Yeah. He's sweet."

"Shelby, you don't understand," Ariel said, grabbing my arm. "He's the first guy to like me in a long time."

"Didn't you have a boyfriend back at school?"

Ariel colored slightly. "Which one—St. Augustine's in Zurich or Fulton Prep in upstate New York or Oceanside

Academy in Orange County?"

"That sucks. It's hard to keep a boyfriend when you keep switching schools."

"Yeah, it doesn't help when they're all-girl schools to start with."

"*No!*" I said, a little too loudly. Everyone stared at me, forgetting all about their dumb raffia birds. *Way to go, Shelby.*

"Problems?" Dr. Wanda was one of those adults who could sneak up on you in milliseconds without any sound.

"She's great. Upset about her crappy wings," Ariel said, holding up my lopsided bird, which was, obviously, not my best work.

"We all have crappy wings. The challenge is to use them to fly," Dr. Wanda said. She gave me a pat on one of my shoulders. "You can do it, Shelby."

"I think I'm gonna puke," Jenna said, making a gagging motion over at the table.

"Oh, just make your bird," I growled at her.

Dr. Wanda walked on, leaving Ariel and me alone.

"You poor thing," I said. "No guys?"

"No," Ariel said. "I'm not sure what to do about Price." She met my eyes for a second, looking slightly embarrassed, and then started straightening one of her bird's legs.

"You don't do anything, okay?" I said. "It's just like being friends, but then, one day, you'll know if you really like him, and things change. It happens on its own."

"So, um . . ." She smiled shyly at me. "What do I do if he wants to make out?"

"If you want to do it, then do it," I said. "But be sure it's for real, Ariel."

Chewing her lip, she glanced at me in the mirror. "Is it real with you and Austin? I mean, I think you guys are great together. He's gorgeous. He's talented."

He's a werewolf, I wanted to add.

"Well, he's definitely different from other guys I've known," I said. For half a sec I considered spilling my guts, but of course that would have been a terrible idea.

She shook her head. "Austin's not that different. He's just your average son of a rock star. Trust me, I've known a few."

"Yeah, I guess . . ."

"What's wrong?" Ariel smiled uneasily.

I shook my head. "Nothing."

She sighed. "If you're worried about his problem, just don't get sucked in. Isn't that what Dr. Wanda said yesterday in girls' group? You can only be responsible for yourself."

I took a piece of green raffia and added it to my wings. I thought about that whole wanting-to-help thing I did and about how maybe that was all about taking responsibility for other people and their choices instead of letting them just deal. But what if the other person had no choice? What if you were the only person who got their problem at all? What if that person wasn't even a person? It was way complicated.

"He's got to do it on his own," Ariel said.

"Yeah." I twisted the raffia round and round the bird and avoided looking over at Austin. The thing was, I didn't think he actually needed my help—there wasn't anything I could do for him. He just didn't want to bear his secret on his own anymore. He didn't want to be alone. I looked over at him, building his crooked bird with straw, making it into something artistic and beautiful—and I felt his pain more deeply than ever before.

"Welcome to Camp Crescent's Talent Night!" Mr. Winters's voice boomed across the barnlike gym and the crowd went wild. Well, as wild as campers who'd suffered through another night of bad cooking could go. "We've got a great lineup, campers! Flashlight jugglers, a skit about the counselors—heh-heh—can't wait for that one, also a poetry reading, and so much more! So let's get started!"

Everyone cheered again. I actually clapped, too. I was psyched to see Ariel on stage.

Then Mr. Winters said, "Okay, folks, our first act is a number from our own songstress Cynthia Crumb!"

The cheering stopped. Cynthia trotted out on stage with her guitar and stepped up to the mic. The room filled with the strange first chords of "Beautiful" by Christina Aguilera.

"Where's your guy?" asked Jenna, who had taken a seat next to mine. "Oh, oops—did he dump you or something?"

I gave her a look, which she totally deserved. "You are as bad as Charles. Maybe you guys should go out," I said.

"Actually, he's kind of cute."

I didn't bother pointing out all the flaws in that theory because at that moment Charles slid into the chair on the other side of me. Suddenly, my bad mood got worse.

"Hey," he said casually.

On stage, Cynthia wrapped up her guitar-pop set and, frowning at the audience's lack of reaction, stormed out of the spotlight.

Mr. Winters gave a courtesy clap. "Next is a presentation of *Beauty and the Beast*."

The stage lights came up, revealing the painted background. Again I was struck by the vivid colors and impressionistic style of Austin's artwork. So was the audience, because a hush came over the crowd.

Price strutted onstage. He'd fashioned a beast headdress out of a brown fleece vest, and his face was painted with whiskers and a dark nose. A buzz went through the audience. Although the costume bordered on ridiculous, it was almost cute. "Who's there?" he called.

Ariel entered from stage left, in a red skirt and peasant top and carrying a basket. "It's Belle. Your guest. Where are you hiding?"

"Don't come any closer!" Price said with a growl. "You needn't see me to appreciate the riches of my castle." He crouched down as if to hide.

"That's ridiculous. Show yourself. My father said you are a beast, but . . . he must be . . . exaggerating big-time."

Price gave Ariel a funny look, and I realized she'd forgotten her lines. Price stepped out of the shadows and into the spotlight.

Ariel gasped. "You are not a man at all. You are a hairy beast!"

"It's true. I am a hairy beast. I'm cursed. I must be this way until I find true love," Price said.

There were a few giggles from the crowd.

Price's eyes narrowed. "You must stay here for a fortnight. Only then will you be free to return to your family. I know I'm not like the other men who have sought your hand, but maybe you will come to love me in time." Price sounded so sincere, the audience stopped laughing.

"How can that be?" Ariel said, starting to remember her real lines. "You frighten me. I will never love you."

I winced. The *Beauty and the Beast* thing had been a really bad idea. Austin had been right to skip the play. The last thing he needed was a reminder of how different he was. But I wasn't a Belle, was I? I mean, I wasn't chicken to be around Austin. I cared about him no matter what form he took. Right?

The second the scene was over, I jetted out of there. I had to find him. I wanted to be with him, to make the most of whatever time we had left—or to make a last-ditch effort to get that serum. I didn't want to be at camp without him. And I was pretty sure it wasn't called jumping in after someone when you already had two feet in the pool.

The nearly full moon hung over Camp Crescent like a spotlight, giving everything a silvery blue glow and casting deep, dark shadows. Light and dark, they went together, even when it came to slightly creepy-looking trees. And maybe that's how people are, too. Only sometimes the shadows seem too deep for the light to overcome.

After searching the cabin trail, the volleyball courts, and the back alley of the kitchen, I found Austin sitting under a tree near the infirmary.

He looked up as I came down the path. "How were the amateur theatrics?"

I gave him a smile. "Beastly."

He reached up and pulled me down to sit next to him. "Forgive my rudeness," he said. "I didn't mean to make you suffer through Talent Night alone. I decided to give Winters's office one last look."

I leaned against the tree trunk and threaded my fingers through the grass around me. "You didn't miss much. Honestly, without the singing candelabra, the play's not so hot."

He didn't laugh at my lame joke.

"No luck with Mr. Winters's office, huh?" I asked.

He shook his head and stuffed his hands into the pockets of his black sweatshirt. "It's clear I can't stay here." Pain edged his voice. "I have to go."

"I don't want you to leave," I said softly.

"Why?"

"You're going to make me say it?"

"By all means," he said, a little sparkle in his brown eyes.

"I kind of, you know . . . like you."

"I'm fond of you, too," he said. He moved closer to me, the centimeters between us dissolving into millimeters, until he was . . .

Tingling with fear, I pulled back, my lips almost warm from the near kiss.

Austin frowned. "I won't bite you. Trust me."

That hit me with extra force. I wanted to kiss him, but I couldn't. Austin was dangerous—and not just in the wild animal category. If I allowed him to like me, to kiss me, who knows what stupid thing I'd do for him? What risk I'd take that would get me in further trouble, when all I needed to do was do my time at Camp Crescent. And stay out of trouble. And I was hardly hanging on to that plan with all these trips into the dark. It wasn't good.

"I do trust you," I said, moving my face into the shadows so he wouldn't see the lie in my expression.

"That's complete rubbish," Austin said. "I've trusted you with my life, my secret. Why won't you trust me?" His gaze firmly fastened to mine, and I felt that weakness in me rise again. The weakness for boys with charming smiles who loved to accompany me down the wrong path while pretending it was the right one.

"I've had too many of these 'trust me' talks lately in my life," I said. "I don't trust you. I don't trust anybody. I don't even trust myself." Ooh, that was weird to say aloud. I wondered where that'd come from, but somehow I knew deep down it was so true.

"Sometimes you have to take a leap of faith. That's what life is. It's a series of leaps."

"I'm not afraid of those."

"But you're afraid of me. You're afraid to kiss me." He reached for my hand. "Life is too short to be afraid to trust people who care about you."

I was afraid. Jillian Montrose was still in the back of my mind. Had Austin told me the whole truth? There was no way for me to know.

Confusion and warmth seemed to radiate throughout my body as he wrapped his arms around me, drawing me closer. I rested my head on his shoulder, taking in the spicy scent of his soap and skin. He still smelled almost like marshmallows. I was pretty sure no killer smelled like that. I sighed into his neck.

"Now if you were a bloody vampire, it'd be all over for me," he whispered, kissing the top of my head.

I sighed and pressed my lips against his skin, feeling his pulse beating beneath. My mouth tingled with warmth. I wanted to kiss him, but that would be . . .

"Not a good idea," I said, pulling away from Austin. "This is a bad, bad idea."

"Don't run from me. I don't want our last night together to end like this."

"It doesn't have to be our last night."

Austin's voice softened. "It's the only thing I can do to protect everyone and myself. I'll be perfectly at home in the forest. It's the best place for me."

"But . . ." I almost said, *What about me?* Really. I actually thought about myself and how it was going to feel to have Austin permanently gone.

He seemed to sense it because he said, "You could walk me to the fence tomorrow after lunch, when we're supposed to be in arts and crafts. The other night I found a hole big enough to fit through. It's a last resort, but I'm afraid I have to take it."

"You realize I can't save you again. If you're lost in the woods this time you're on your own."

"You hardly saved me last time," he said with a smile. "Don't worry, I nicked a map from Charles. Had it hidden in his pillowcase. I'll change at night, but I can recover and hike during the day. By the time I reach the nearest town, the full-moon phase will be over, and I'll be a regular bloke again."

"What if they go looking for you?"

"Oh, I'm sure they will, but you know how they try to keep things hush-hush around here. It'll be Winters and Sven at the most, hardly a threat. I'll smell them coming for me and hike in a different direction."

"When you get to a town? Then what?" I asked, that empty feeling starting again.

"At the town I make a collect call to the chemist in London, have him wire me money and FedEx my serum while I hang out in the local hotel."

It sounded like a terrible plan. He was running. From camp. From me. I could feel tears brewing. "I've gotta go."

"Shelby," Austin said, reaching for my hand again. "If things were different, if I could stay . . ."

"I know. Life sucks," I said coolly.

"Don't forget to meet me tomorrow," Austin whispered.

"Yeah." I stood up and walked down the path alone. Alone wasn't anything new to me. And I knew it wasn't anything new to Austin, either.

I just didn't expect it to hurt so bad.

TWELVE

When I got to girls' group the next morning, most of the girls were already there and Dr. Wanda was riffling through papers at her makeshift desk in the corner, no doubt preparing to lead another scintillating discussion.

Ariel patted the seat next to her. "You missed breakfast," she said.

"Felt sick when I woke up," I explained. I left out the part about not wanting to get out of bed, not wanting this day to start because it was my last day with Austin. Actually, last morning with him, since he'd be bailing after lunch. Who knew if I'd ever see him again? Once he was loose in the woods, he was out of my life, probably forever. That made me incredibly sad.

"Today we'll be writing letters home to express everything we're learning here at camp. I want you to choose the person you communicate the least with in your family to receive the letter."

Groans sounded around the circle.

Dr. Wanda held up a hand like she was warding off the negative comments. "I want you to write the letter as if you would die tomorrow. Tell that person everything you've always wanted to say."

I raised my hand. "How're we supposed to pick the person?"

"You pick the person you can't talk to," Jenna said, breaking it down as if she'd done it a hundred times at a hundred other brat camps. "The one who really needs to hear you."

"Okay, so what if you don't talk to *anyone* in your family?" Ariel said.

Dr. Wanda let out an exasperated sigh. "Choose a family member with whom you'd like to communicate better."

I raised my hand again and said, "What if you—"

"Just pick someone!" Dr. Wanda said, completely losing her cool. "I'm sorry," she added after noticing our shocked faces. "This week at camp is always tough. Does anyone want to talk about their feelings?"

"I felt hurt when you screamed at us," Sue, a big girl, said.

Dr. Wanda frowned. "No, I mean—"

"I felt betrayed," said Callie, the thin blond girl from my cabin.

"You really did hurt my feelings," Sue complained.

Dr. Wanda ran a hand through her frizzy black bangs, trying to smooth them, when it was obvious only some leave-in conditioner would have any kind of positive effect. "Girls, I'm proud that you're developing the emotional vocabulary we've been working on." She took a breath. "Shall we concentrate on writing those letters now?"

Everyone shut up after that and got to work, writing on the sheets of cheap notebook paper Wanda passed out.

"Who should I write to?" I whispered to Ariel.

"How should I know?" she whispered back.

"Shh!" said Jenna, tears rolling down her skinny cheeks. "I'm trying to write here."

I gaped at her. She'd gone from zero to sobbing in, like, two minutes. *Okay . . .*

"Who are *you* writing to?" I said, leaning Ariel's way again.

"My mother," she said. "She lives on Park Avenue with her new boyfriend, Kip Kensington. He's that dweeb from that stupid game show. Makes Alex Trebek look studly," she added with a shrug. "Just pick your mom. It'll be easy."

Since my conversation with Austin the other night, I actually had been thinking about my mom. Take away all the therapy junk and werewolf issues, and this camp would have been somewhere my mom would have loved. Even when she'd been really sick from chemo, Mom used to have Dad help her to the bench in our backyard garden so she could watch the sunset. She really dug nature stuff.

"You okay?" Ariel was staring at me because obviously I'd zoned out thinking about Mom.

"Yeah, um, the thing is . . . my mom's dead," I said quietly, so only Ariel could hear.

It felt weird to tell her that. I totally expected to see pity in her eyes, but when Ariel looked at me there was only kindness.

"That sucks," she said. "That really, really sucks."

"Yeah."

"You should've told me. I mean, all that stuff I said about Austin's mother," she said gently. "If I'd known . . ."

I managed a little smile because I didn't want her feeling like crap or anything. "It's okay. Really."

Ariel nodded, then glanced down at her paper. "So, um, what about your stepmother?"

"Ugh. Priscilla, a.k.a. Honey Bun."

"Write to her. Look." She pointed at Dr. Wanda, slowly moving from girl to girl around the circle toward us. "Just choose someone."

"Okay, okay." Right then I wrote the date on the top of my paper and then doodled in the margins, pretending to write, but really I thought about how I was so relieved Ariel didn't make a big deal out of my mom. For some reason it felt good that she knew. And that Austin knew. Neither one had drowned me in pity.

"You could still write to your mom," Ariel said, looking up from her half-completed page. "That would be kinda cool, you know?"

"Yeah, maybe," I said. Then I saw how she was totally right. Writing to my mom, even though she'd never be able to read the letter, would be way better than writing to Priscilla, the one person I never spoke to at home.

Then again . . .

I paused, chewing the eraser on the end of the pencil. That stuff about Priscilla was totally wrong; I was pretty much forced to talk to her a lot. She was the one who criticized my outfits in the morning, demanded to see my homework, screamed at me to get off my cell phone and to come down to eat my so-called dinner.

But Dad? It was almost funny how far away he felt most of the time. If he wasn't working late at his lab, he was snoring in the family room in front of Discovery Channel specials (mostly on snakes, ugh!). He barely noticed if I got my hair cut, tried to sneak another piercing, or was wearing green nail polish in honor of Saint Paddy's Day.

Mom may have died, but Dad was the real missing person in my life.

Suddenly, the pencil seemed smaller in my hand, or else I was gripping it really tight. I didn't know that I'd ever give him this letter, but I started with the words "Dear Dad."

When Dr. Wanda called out it was time for lunch, I glanced down and my eyes almost bugged out of my head. I'd filled two pages. Two pages of all the things I'd wanted to tell him, the things I thought he should have done, the things I wished he'd asked me. I wasn't telling this to anybody he paid to talk to me—I was telling him.

Dr. Wanda patted me on the shoulder as I set down my pen. "It feels good to get it all out, doesn't it?"

I didn't want her to think she'd actually done something that'd kinda helped, but I had to nod. It did feel good. Well, weird but good. It was, like, for once I was talking and no one was interrupting me or asking stupid questions. Me writing it all down was like my dad was listening to me. Maybe if we had tried harder to talk to each other since Mom died, I wouldn't have had so much to write. Seriously. Maybe I wouldn't have even been there in that stupid camp in the first place.

"Do you want me to mail that for you?" asked Dr. Wanda.

I shook my head. "Um, I'll hang on to it," I said, folding the letter into a tiny square.

"That's perfectly fine." Dr. Wanda gave me a warm smile and walked back to her desk with a stack of notes to mail.

Ariel told me one time that her mom admitted something important in a mother-daughter therapy session: Adults don't always get everything right. So my question is, if they aren't always right, then how can we be the ones who're getting everything wrong?

Maybe both sides make choices that don't turn out to be the smartest. But if you're afraid to make mistakes, you can't learn, right? Maybe that was where I had something my dad didn't. I'd taken some risks, and I'd definitely messed up. I was kind of fearless in that department. At least I had been until I got to camp. There were consequences here—like Red Canyon—that totally sucked.

Of course, there had been consequences at home, but I'd ignored them. I hadn't taken them seriously. I'd broken rules just because. And I was starting to think that wasn't being fearless, it was being stupid. I mean, what had been the point of any of it? To get my dad's attention? To show Priscilla I wasn't afraid of her, when obviously she didn't care what I thought? What a waste of time.

I shoved the letter into my pocket and walked out of the classroom into the glaring light of the summer day. I wasn't sure I'd ever mail that note to Dad, but I felt like something in me had changed.

Just after lunch, it was time to say good-bye to Austin and get back to living my normally scheduled werewolf-free life, so I took the path toward the cabins like I was going back to get something before arts and crafts. Halfway there, I veered off onto the smaller trail, which led to where I was supposed to meet Austin. The trail wound through evergreens, and in the distance to my right, I could see the outline of some of the cabins. I breathed in the piney scent no floor cleaner could ever copy along with the warm earthy smell of things growing. Summer smelled so good, even at brat camp.

It was warm, so I slipped off my red zip sweatshirt and tied it around my waist. As I moved farther into the woods, the trail cut to the left through ferns, huckleberry bushes, and dense rows of scrubby firs. I battled through the vegetation, my bare legs taking a fair share of scratches. At last the path got really narrow, like an animal had made it. Standing in a clearing twenty yards ahead was Austin.

"Brilliant," he said, smiling widely. His amber brown eyes always looked amazing, but today they reflected bits of the green forest around us. I took a mental picture in case I never saw him again.

"You didn't think I'd leave you hanging," I said.

"I hoped you wouldn't. I wasn't certain."

I gulped back the nervous feeling in my throat and said, "Um, I know you like meat, but here's some gum I got from Price, and here're two oatmeal cookies I saved from lunch. I figured you might get hungry, you know, before the moon shines."

Austin took my gifts, looking happily surprised.

I fished a piece of paper from my pocket and shoved it in his free hand. "So . . . there's my number if you want to call me."

He stared at me, not moving. I couldn't read the emotion on his face, but it kinda looked like complete shock and horror.

Oh, man. I was a total dork—it was official. The absolute uncoolest way to say good-bye ever. Giving my cell number to a werewolf? Total insanity.

Austin folded the paper small in his hand. "I'll ring you at the end of the summer. I promise."

I nodded. Now that I felt like an idiot, I wanted Austin to, like, run off. "Okay, so good luck."

"Wait. That's not a proper good-bye," Austin said, brushing his bangs out of his eyes. "Come here, you." He caught me by the hand, bringing me toward him.

Okay, so maybe I wasn't an idiot or a dork. I licked my bottom lip, wishing for real I had some lip gloss because Austin was going to kiss me, and kiss me good. It would be all right because it was a good-bye kiss, I told myself. It was totally safe.

For a moment he stood there, looking at me. "Thank you," he said finally, his low rumbly voice and his accent making the two simple words sound like music.

My heart pitter-pattered in my chest. It was unnerving staring into Austin's eyes. He was more than a boy—he was also a beautiful, dangerous creature.

"You're welcome," I managed to say. "I was just doing what I'd hope someone would do for me in that kind of situation, you know?"

He dipped his head closer. The heat of his breath feathered against my cheek. I licked my lips again and tried to remain calm. And standing. I tried to remain standing. The swoony feeling in my legs was getting worse, and there wasn't a tree trunk in sight to lean against. I'd been waiting for this kiss and terrified of it at the same time. And now it was here.

"You're beautiful," Austin said. "I never got a chance to tell you that."

"Oh." My legs drooped a little. Swoon alert! "Um, thanks."

"No, thank you. For everything." He moved in to kiss me, but stopped halfway to my lips. He raised his head, sniffing at the air.

I've had guys do lots of weird things in the middle of trying to kiss me—answer their cell phone, wave at their friends, even take a bite of a double-cheeseburger—but sniff? Was it me? Oh, no. Had I pitted out my T-shirt or something? I tilted my head to smell myself without him noticing. Whew. I was good.

"Um, Austin?"

He whirled around on the trail. "Shelby, we have to hide. Someone's coming." He sniffed the air again. "Bloody Charles."

"I'll run back down the trail."

"No, it's better if he doesn't see you. There's no reason to endanger yourself."

Austin was looking out for me. Nice.

"Good point," I said.

"Come on, there are trees this way." Austin pulled me down the trail. The chain-link fence loomed twenty yards ahead of us. Unattached fencing curled away from one of the support poles, making a hole big enough for Austin to crawl through.

But I had to hide. The only trees I saw in front of the fence were scrubby. They wouldn't hide a garden gnome.

"I thought you said there were trees?"

Austin shushed me. "He's moving faster. I hear him closing in. I have to go." He peeled back the fence and ducked through.

"Um, um," I said, glancing around in a bit of a panic. Crap! What was I supposed to do, run? I considered those gnome trees, but they just weren't gonna cut it.

"You haven't any time," Austin said.

"Fine! I'll hide over there." There were some thick-trunked trees on the other side of the fence. I'd take my chances with them, then scurry back over.

Austin helped me through and then rolled the metal back, so it looked like it was all in one piece. Then he grabbed my hand and pulled me toward the trees. Once we'd picked a huge, leafy alder, Austin pointed back at the trail.

Footsteps clomping like a horse, Charles bounded toward us. "I know you're out here, lovebirds."

"What an idjit," Austin muttered.

"Shh." I hugged the tree, acutely aware of Austin's body next to mine, his breath on my cheek.

"Once you go over the fence it's over, Shelby," Charles taunted, threading through the bushes. "Do you want to end up worse than Jillian Montrose?"

Austin's jaw clenched. He looked ready to pop out and smack Charles.

"Don't fall for it," I whispered.

"Or maybe you're already on the other side of the fence? Have you made a break for it? Well, an attack in the woods would make a great story. If you survive, I could get you the cover of *Celebrities Exposed* for a tell-all interview." Charles moved closer to the fence, looking like he was about to peel it back and come through himself, when sounds echoed through the woods—jingling metal and someone plodding through the thick brush.

"Charles! So Cynthia was right!" Mr. Winters's booming voice called out. "She saw you loitering around the trailhead."

"Bloody hell," Austin said under his breath.

"Shh," I said. I needed Mr. Winters to go away so I could sneak back down the trail.

Austin nodded, pulling me closer to him against the trunk of the tree. I counted to ten while Charles and Mr. Winters argued, holding my breath. The last thing we needed was for them to see us.

"There *is* a break in the fence," Mr. Winters was saying. "But I don't see anyone but you, Charles. How did you say you happened upon this break in the fence? We're clearly in an off-limits area."

"I told you," cried Charles. "I followed Austin the other night."

Austin squirmed. I placed a hand on his arm to remind him there was still a chance they might see us.

Mr. Winters went on. "When you were out walking after lights-out? That's a day of community service—let's say peeling potatoes for the cook this time?"

"But Austin was—"

"I'd be happy to talk to him later so he can refute your story."

"But the fence," Charles said in a defeated tone.

"That's not a problem," Mr. Winters replied, followed by a heavy clunking noise. "I came prepared."

Austin and I traded glances and then slowly peered around our tree trunk. Oh, crap. There was a toolbox on the ground next to Mr. Winters, who was taking out some kind of pliers thing. I watched in horror as he twisted the fence's metal strands firmly back together.

"No one is escaping out this hole. No one," Mr. Winters

said, grunting with effort, "without wire cutters, that is."

"You don't understand," Charles whined. "It's probably too late!"

"Sure, son." Mr. Winters finished the repair and then led away Charles, who was trying to argue his way out of kitchen duty. When they were gone, we ran to the fence.

"Oh, no!" I said, shaking the chain link.

"Don't panic," Austin said, checking the strength of the repair.

Meanwhile, I scoped out the top and wondered how cut up my legs might get from the barbed wire. "Maybe I could climb—"

"You can't do it, Shelby," Austin said. "The fence is secure. You're stuffed."

"If that means I'm screwed, I think you're right." I sat down on the ground, putting my head between my knees. "I'm stuck in the woods with a werewolf."

THIRTEEN

*D*on't fret. We'll get you back through the fence. Somehow." Austin sat down on the ground next to me and put an arm around my shoulders.

I glanced up at him, startled by his touch. I knew I shouldn't be afraid of him, but I was. I couldn't help it now that the circumstances had changed.

He cleared his throat, making me realize I was staring at him. "If we're going to try something we'd better hurry," he said. "I calculated I'd have about forty-five minutes before I was really missed. With you here, too, we'll have less time."

"When I don't show up at arts and crafts, Ariel is going to freak." I jumped up and shook the fence again. The twisted wires didn't budge. "Piece-of-crap fence!"

"Right. The fence isn't going to work, Shelby. It's two miles to the front gate," Austin said. "We could try going there."

Now I really gave him the evil eye. "The front gate? So I can turn myself in? If I do that I'll really be screwed. The plan was to say good-bye to you, then run back to camp before anyone noticed I was gone. Nothing is working out the way I thought it would."

Austin stuffed his hands in his jeans pockets. "We can't stand here talking for much longer. You have to make a decision. What will it be?"

What could I do? If I went back, I'd be in trouble—Winters would call Priscilla and my summer would be over. If I stayed with Austin, though, there was a chance I could hike out before nightfall, get to a phone, and then . . . nothing. I had nothing. What would I possibly do after that? I'd be a runaway. Not what I wanted to do to get my dad to trust me again.

I sighed. "Let's try for the main gate. Maybe I can slip back in and pretend to have a concussion from a falling rock or something."

"Good plan." He stood there looking at me expectantly.

I poked him in the chest. "Okay, so lead the way. You've got a map, right?"

He bit his lip. "Ah, actually, no. Just a rough sketch from the fence to the forest road in my journal. I returned the original to Charles's bunk. Casting off suspicion and all that. And on principle, I had to return it."

I punched Austin in the shoulder.

"Ouch! What the devil was that for?"

"You left the real map *behind*? What kind of escapee are you?"

"I didn't plan on doubling back to drop you off," he said, rubbing his shoulder.

"Well, which way do you think the gate is?"

"I suppose that way," he said, pointing randomly, it seemed to me.

Resisting the urge to panic, I walked with Austin into the trees, keeping the fence in my line of sight. We were kind of walking in a northward direction, based on the sun's position. But it was only two o'clock, so it wasn't that easy to tell. By the time sunset came, maybe we'd have a better idea of directions. Oh, wait. Sunset? I so hoped we found the front gate before then.

"Um, what time does the moon come out?" I asked casually.

Austin made a growling sound, probably thinking he was being funny. "You don't look remotely appetizing."

"Just watch yourself," I said in what I hoped was a confident tone. And I walked on, keeping one eye on the distant fence and one on Austin, which was really hard to do without tripping.

"This is not good," I said, as if that would somehow help. Below us, in a deep ravine, bushes, ferns, and a collection of fallen trees and sharp-looking sticks masked a small creek. There didn't seem to be any way around, and I was so not balancing on some half-rotten log to cross it.

"Not to worry," Austin said. We'd been walking for about three hours, according to his watch. The road and gate hadn't materialized, but Austin was still acting like he knew the way. It was getting old.

"Hmm . . . This wasn't on the map," Austin said, scratching at his long bangs. "We must have taken a wrong turn somewhere."

"A wrong turn?" I leaned a hand against the nearest tree. "Dude. I have to get to the gate! No one is ever going to believe the whole concussion story if I don't do it now! I mean, soon they'll probably be out here with, like, hounds or something to chase us down. I'm *so* going to Red Canyon."

"Red Canyon?"

"The hell of brat camps, Austin! My witch of a stepmother is going to send me there the minute she gets wind of this."

"You were merely trying to help me," Austin said. "You weren't trying to run away. Surely she'd—"

"No. She won't be reasonable. The woman doesn't have a shred of reason in her stupid skinny body."

"I was going to say, surely she'd listen to your side of it," Austin said, frowning at me. "Mind you, *I'm* not the adversary here."

I stood there fuming. "She won't listen to me. No one ever does."

Austin's expression softened. He slung his backpack off his shoulder and sat down on the nearest stump. "I'm sorry I got you into this."

I plunked down next to him. "You didn't force me through the fence, Austin. It was totally my stupid idea."

"Well, if I hadn't been—"

171

"It's my own fault," I said. I closed my eyes and rested, trying to forget that I had no clue what we'd do next. After a while, though, the bubbling sound of a nearby creek made me thirsty. "Can I have some water?"

"Sure." Austin reached into his bag and groaned. "The water bottle, Shelby. You didn't cap it after your last drink."

"I did," I said.

"Apparently not well enough." He pulled the bottle out and held it up for me to see the drips running down its sides.

"Oh, great," I said. "I doubt you thought to bring a portable water filter. We'll die of thirst out here."

"Wait. That's only the beginning." Austin set the bottle on the ground and pulled his journal from his bag. Black drops dripped from it onto the dirt.

"No-oo!" I cried. "Haven't you ever heard of waterproof ink?"

Austin's eyes narrowed. "I hardly expected anyone to put an open bottle of water into my pack."

My face got hot. "It wasn't open. I mean, I thought I closed the bottle," I explained.

"I'd say it was halfway closed." He laid the book reverently down on some ferns and opened the pages.

The water damage was pretty severe. Page after soggy page ran with ink from beautiful drawings of birds. The most beautiful smeary bird pictures I'd ever seen.

"Austin, those are amazing."

He shrugged but also looked pleased at the same time. "Even

with medication, most nights before a full moon I can't sleep. I draw by candlelight to pass the time. Luckily, Sven didn't find the candles and extra matches hidden in my shoes."

"Oh, crap." I pointed down at the journal. "The map?"

Sighing, Austin flipped toward a page in the back of the book. Water had only slightly smeared the hand-drawn map. Of course, it was toward the slightly smeared part that we'd been heading.

"Well, there's no ravine," I said. "Even with the smudges, I can see that."

"Yes. I'd say we're lost," Austin said.

"Can't you, like, use your wolfy senses? You know, to smell the way to camp or civilization?"

"My senses help, but they don't work that way. If I'm tracking someone, I search out their scent, but I need a reference scent, a starting point. Trying to remember a scent isn't as effective."

"And you've never smelled the town where we're going," I said. "So you can't sniff that out."

"Where we're going? You're going with me?" Austin said, his voice a little concerned.

"Duh! If I can't find camp, then I have to go on toward the town."

He let out a big sigh. "That presents a whole new problem, doesn't it?"

"What? I've come all this way with you, and you don't want me to go to town with you?"

Austin brushed a piece of bark from the knee of his jeans. "It's not that."

"Then what?" I said, getting madder by the second.

"It's only that—"

"Holy crap! You're worried that you'll go wolfy and attack me."

"No." Austin let out a long, deep sigh. "Actually, I'm more worried about frightening you than anything else." He opened his mouth and pointed to his teeth. His canines seemed whiter and larger.

I gaped at him, not knowing what to say.

He closed his mouth, looking embarrassed. "It's a precursor to the natural lunar change for some of us. The rest of the transformation happens rapidly."

"I won't freak out," I said, hoping I sounded reassuring.

"You don't know that," Austin said.

"And, hey, at least we're not back at camp burning those stupid raffia birds with Dr. Wanda."

He managed a weak smile. "You're not coming with me, Shelby."

"Look," I said, "we'll find a naughty woodchuck who really deserves a horrible death. You'll get a snack, and everything'll be golden." I tried to laugh, but it came out all hysterical-sounding. It felt lame to be making jokes.

And Austin's dead-serious expression made me realize that looking on the bright side wasn't going to save me if I came face-to-face with a hungry wolf.

Hours later, the oranges and reds of the sunset cast a glow on the trees and rocks around us. It was beautiful except for the pale moon rising like a bluish white ghost at the other side of the horizon.

We'd been hiking in what seemed to me a random direction, and my patience was almost totally gone. I was tired, hungry, and worried. For about the millionth time, we paused so Austin could squint down at the smeared map.

This time he looked up smiling. "That must be the hill. You should find the camp entrance on the other side."

I clapped my hands together. "Sweet. Are you sure?"

"Yes. According to what's left of my diagram, it's not far." He ran a hand through his long bangs, smoothing them back behind his ears. His hair gleamed against the sunset, making me think of that time I'd seen him at the river, a part of all the natural surroundings. How right I'd been. He really was more than handsome, he was beautiful.

"What is it? A mosquito?" he said, slapping at his cheeks.

I smiled. "No, no. I'm just, um, thinking about that first day."

"You mean last week."

I tried to focus on him without losing myself in his amber eyes, which were, at the moment, blazing with all the sky colors. "It seems like forever ago, doesn't it?"

He nodded, and somehow there we were, staring into each other's eyes. I got a funny sinking feeling in my belly. Not the kind that happens when you're all disappointed or something, but that kind of falling feeling like when you're going down fast in an elevator.

Austin cleared his throat all nervouslike and then said, "It does seem like forever." His eyelashes fluttered for a moment, and my mind flashed to what he'd said at the fence about me—that I was beautiful. I almost believed it, the way he was looking at me.

"So . . . right. Off you go," he said. "You've got my candles and matches if you need them. I'm sorry I haven't a torch for you. As long as you can, keep walking with the sunset on your left side."

"Duh, you mean north," I said, shaking my head. "Don't worry. I'm excellent in the woods," I told him.

"I haven't a doubt."

"And you're sure you're not going to chase me down and feast on my bloodied corpse?" I said with a weak smile.

"Trust me." Ooh, those words echoed in my brain for a minute. *Trust me*, the root of all boy evil.

"That didn't really work for Little Red Riding Hood," I said.

"Do I look like the Big Bad Wolf?" said Austin with a slow smile.

"Not yet, but there's not exactly a woodcutter to save me, anyway."

He paused. "You're not about letting other people save you, Shelby. Even I can see that."

Hmm. He had me there. Did that mean he thought I was, like, brave? Both he and Mr. Winters had said stuff about that.

176

I'd always thought of myself as kinda fearless, but in a reckless way, you know? Brave and fearless are totally not the same thing. Brave is like being fearless for an actual reason.

"I don't want to leave you," I said, sticking my hands in the pockets of my sweatshirt.

"Shelby, be realistic. Here's where we separate. Head up that path there, the rocky one that cuts through those skinny trees at the top of the hill. Like *you* said, I'll be fine."

I shrugged like it was no big deal, but I *was* worried about him. I'd been worried about him from the start.

Austin wrapped his arms around me and held me tightly. All the sparks inside me collided, and I felt a scared but secure feeling. How could I feel so safe with someone who was so dangerous? What was wrong with me?

He kissed the top of my head. "I'll be in touch again, I promise. I won't forget you." He loosened his grip on me and used a hand to lift my chin so we were looking eye to eye. "Straightaway to camp, now. Don't look back."

And there it was. The moment I'd been dreading and hoping for all in one. Our first and probably last ever kiss.

A sad look took over his eyes. "I know you're afraid, so I'll just . . ." he said, lowering his lips. And then moving to my cheek. His lips were hot like a brand, and for a moment I felt my knees weaken. But then I felt something scratch my cheek. One of Austin's sharp teeth.

I broke away from him, knowing it was time to leave.

FOURTEEN

I had only walked up the hill a little ways when I had the irresistible urge to glance back. Just to make sure Austin was there by that tree while I could still make him out in the distance. The moon, so pale it was almost translucent, hung over the top of the trees near where we'd stood. It was full and huge. I shivered at the sight.

Then I saw Austin in the middle of the clearing to the side of the trees, spotlighted by the embers of sunset. He was turned sideways, his face lifted toward the rising moon. It was like he was caught between day and night—between wolf and regular guy.

I didn't think he could see me, but I crouched down behind a big rock anyway, watching him. Call it stupid curiosity or whatever, but I wanted to see him change.

Ah-ooooooooohh! A howl shook the little valley, echoing so much that I wasn't sure at first where it came from.

Ah-oooooooohh! This cry I could tell came from Austin because his back arched with effort and then his body crumpled to a heap in the tall grass.

I gasped, worried about what was happening to him, yet I wasn't motivated in the least to run down and check. In fact, I wasn't motivated to move an inch from behind that rock. As if agreeing with the whole staying-put idea, my feet felt as heavy as weights.

Ah-oooooooohh! Another howl sounded, this one higher pitched and eerie. The tall grass rippled where Austin had fallen. There was a flash of skin, his arm maybe. Then the blue of his jeans streaked by, as if being tossed away. Another howl rose, followed by some yipping.

Uh-oh. I forced myself to release the breath I'd been holding. This whole thing was real. He was totally changing into something. It was time to start hiking—like, really really fast—but it was so hard to tear myself away from the amazing scene below me.

Just then something dark brown rose in the grass.

"Holy crap," I muttered, rubbing at my eyes.

Ears, wolf ears. Then a whole head. A canine head pointed in the direction of the hill. My direction.

My heart hammered in my chest, and not in a good way. Austin saw me. I mean, the *wolf* saw me, because that's what he was now, stalking through the tall grass. A beautiful dark brown and black wolf as big as a Great Dane.

I scrambled up and then, in an attempt to combine running

for my life and hiking, totally tripped over my own feet. I dusted myself off and ran, glancing back one more time.

The wolf was gone. Gone from my sight, anyway. But I couldn't be sure he wasn't on his way up the hill right now. I started blazing through the trees, not caring that night was smothering the forest like a dark blue blanket.

I really hoped Austin had been right about the hill leading to Camp Crescent. Otherwise . . . man, I didn't even want to think about otherwise.

A candle makes a super crappy flashlight. I was already on my third one and had at least ten wax burns on my hands to show for it. Near the summit of the hill that supposedly led to camp, I held the stub of the current candle out in front of me and kept pushing through the dense evergreens. So far, I'd remained pretty calm, considering, but when a breeze ruffled some trees off to the side of me I about had a heart attack.

Chill, I told myself. *You can totally do this.* With my free hand, I pulled my sweatshirt a little tighter around me and walked, focusing on the trail ahead. At last, there was a break in the trees and I stood at the top of a long, winding trail that led downhill. Moonlight shone on the path, which looked like hard-packed dirt, a welcome change from the rocky mess that'd led up the hill. *See, I knew you could do it,* my brain gloated. *You're almost there.* Feeling a little more confident, I charged ahead on the path.

Grrrrrrr-rrrr! A low growl sounded, followed by a kind of screeching noise.

All the hairs on my body stood up. Oh, crap. Austin was coming after me.

I turned slowly, almost afraid to look. The bushes behind me swayed ever so slightly. But not enough to make me think there was anything there. I exhaled and turned back around, taking a step.

Ah-oooooooohh!

My hair did the standing-on-end thing again. *Austin?* I froze, listening as the echo of the howl died away. Then, reluctantly, I looked over my shoulder. The bushes swayed again, then stopped.

I felt a breeze against my cheek. Just a breeze. I pulled the hood of my red sweatshirt up. Then, telling myself again to chill, I started down the path.

Probably a half hour later, reaching the base of the hill, I expected to find the magical gate to Camp Crescent. From what Austin had described, it was supposed to be right there. Instead, I found another stupid ravine.

As best I could make out with my puny candle and the streams of moonlight, below me was a gorge cut into the freaking forest, complete with another creek bubbling by all happy. I started lowering myself down the steep side of the ravine, clinging onto roots and big rocks. I was maybe twenty feet down when I heard it.

Grrrrrr-rrrr!

My hair follicles, of course, did their creeped-out thing. And my feet slipped a little in the loose dirt of the bank. I dropped a few feet lower.

A screech ripped through the darkness. I scrambled down the bank, knowing there wasn't time to lift myself up to the ledge where I'd been standing a moment before. As stickery vines tore at my legs on the way down, I cursed the short-shorts I was wearing. Finally, I landed on the ground, my feet splashing into the creek.

The screech sounded again, giving me serious goose bumps. Werewolves really weren't just wolves, I thought, glancing up at the ledge. They were a whole new kind of scary beast. Very scary-sounding beasts.

The rocks were slippery and hard to see, since my candle was barely going anymore and the moonlight hardly reached this ravine. My Nikes were sopping wet when I reached the other side of the creek.

Glancing back over my shoulder, I didn't see anything coming, but I heard yipping again, like coyotes barking or something. I shuddered, kicking my way through grass and low bushes until I came to the opposite bank of the ravine. It was as steep as the other side had been, so I reached out with my free hand for the nearest exposed root and hauled myself upward. I dug my toes into the dirt, trying to make little holds, but mostly just loosened soil and rocks.

Grrrrrrr-rrrr!

Holy crap. That sounded like it came from right behind me. I scrabbled at the dirt with my free hand till I had a good grip and forced my body up a few feet. Then my toes finally found a good spot. When I hoisted myself up again, I was farther up the bank, about halfway.

Grrrrrrr-rrrr!

I glanced over my shoulder and saw something dark prowling through the bushes like it was stalking me. I suddenly thought about what I must look like, me in my red hooded sweatshirt. Being followed by a Big Bad Wolf. Nice.

"I knew it! I totally knew it!" I couldn't help shouting out because it pissed me off that I was about to be werewolf chow. "You suck!"

The thing in the bushes stopped.

I crammed my hands into the dirt again and hauled myself up a few more feet. Man, either my arms were weak or my skinny butt was heavy. The heck with the elliptical machine in the family room at home, I was so getting a personal trainer if I ever made it out alive.

The slope started to get less slanted, which was a great thing, because when I looked down, the four-legged beast had reached the creek. It was shadowy down there—well, it was shadowy everywhere. My little candle had totally gone out on the way up the cliff, and anyway, it wasn't like you could project a stupid candle flicker to light up a creek bed. But I could soon tell that the thing below me was definitely

183

a wolf because little slivers of moonlight cut through the canopy of tree branches, highlighting him.

"Austin?" I paused for a moment to fully scope out what he'd become.

His head was enormous and beautiful in kind of a terrifying way. His tongue hung out of one edge of his wide mouth as he panted. Gleaming golden in the faint light, Austin's eyes seemed the only recognizable part of him. He was way bigger than he'd seemed from a distance during the change. He made a low guttural sound, staring me down.

My blood turned to ice in my veins. "Nice doggie," I said. Not like I thought that was going to work or anything, but I was on the verge of puking or peeing myself, so I had to do something.

The wolf stepped into the creek, his gaze still on me.

Oh, crap. I groped for some kind of heavy stick or something but only felt more of the vines I'd been using to help me climb. Turning around so I could keep him in my sight, I gripped the vines the best I could and then started climbing the ravine cliff backward like a frightened crab.

He splashed easily through the creek, issuing that warning sound again. I made it to the top of the cliff as he reached the base of the slope. Panicking, I scrambled through the bushes, my heart pumping like crazy. Any second, I was toast, and not in the romantic, moonlight way.

Ah-oooooooohh! A howl reverberated from the ravine.

Was this the last shred of his humanity telling me to run? I gladly took his advice. The branches cut into my already scraped-up arms and legs, but I kept pushing through the thick trees to get as far away from him as I could. Up here on the ridge, a clear shot to the moon, the whole forest was lit up electric blue, making it easier to see. Still, breathing raggedly, I crashed through a patch of stinging nettles, yelping as I made contact.

Then the screech sounded again. From what direction, I couldn't say. It was almost like it was in front of me, or beside me. I didn't stop to check it out. I kept running.

As I rounded a bend in the trail, I heard movement behind me. When I looked over my shoulder, I saw Austin bounding through the trees. A dark blur, he was gaining on me.

"*Ahhhhh!*" I screamed as he caught up.

But then he rocketed past me. With a growl that about curled my wavy hair, he dove into the tall bushes in front of me. The screech sounded again. The bush shook, crashing sounds and growling rumbling out of it.

A second later, Austin tumbled out of the bush with another four-legged creature. I couldn't be sure, but it didn't look like another wolf. I dropped to the ground, totally freaked.

The other creature let out a screech. A screech I recognized as the sound from the hill when we'd first separated. *Austin hadn't been following me—he'd been stalking that thing—which had been stalking me!*

With a snarl, Austin went for his opponent's throat. It was a large cat—maybe a cougar. Whatever the heck it was, it was vicious. It swiped at Austin with its huge paws, making contact with Austin's shoulder.

Austin yelped and jumped backward. Then, teeth gnashing, he lunged at the cat. This time he had the cat by the neck and he swung it around. The cat's cry made my teeth hurt, like nails on a chalkboard.

The thing clawed at Austin's neck, hitting the shoulder wound again, but Austin kept fighting. He snapped at the cat, his jaws foaming. The cat reared back and then, with one last screech, jetted off into the bushes.

Austin wobbled upright for a moment, then slumped to the ground.

"No!" I screamed, rushing toward him. He couldn't be dead. He just couldn't be. But Austin wasn't moving.

Shaking because I didn't know what he might do while still in his wolf form, I knelt down a few yards from Austin. Bathed in a pool of moonlight, he was still breathing, his chest rising and falling in an irregular pattern. The gash on his shoulder looked deep, though—dark beads of blood welled beside it.

The forest seemed to close in around us—acres and acres of trees and bushes and God knows what else was out there hiding. Maybe the cat would come back to finish off both of us. He probably had a bunch of hungry friends, too. And all Austin had to fend away more attackers was me. Tears of frustration rolled down my cheeks. I forced myself to move closer to the wolf.

I could see he was bleeding like crazy—and I was scared to reach out and touch him. I was scared of the wolf. And I was scared because he was going to bleed to death and then I really would never see Austin again.

The wolf whimpered as his furry body shook with some kind of convulsion. My heart lurched in my chest. If I didn't do anything, then he really might die. *Come on, Shelby—suck it up, be brave,* I told myself. *Be brave when it counts.*

I didn't know anything about wolves, but I did know from basic first aid I had to stop the bleeding from his shoulder wound. I knelt beside him and bit the hem of my baby T, tearing the bottom of the shirt off into a long strip. With trembling hands I reached out with the fabric, knowing I had to touch him. I had to trust him—and myself.

His wolf ears pricked up like he knew I was there, but he didn't move his head.

I pressed the material to his bloody shoulder.

Snap! His head jerked toward me. I felt a stinging on my forearm. He'd grazed me with his teeth.

"It's me, Austin," I said, pulling back to rub the spot on my arm. It smarted, but it wasn't bleeding. "It's okay. I'm going to help you." I wadded the T-shirt material in my hand again and held it to the wound.

This time, Austin's wolf body seemed to relax. He made another whimpering noise, like the pressure hurt, but I didn't move my hand. I had to stop the bleeding. I just hoped that would be enough.

FIFTEEN

*S*helby?"

I opened my eyes. The sky above was faint gold with sunrise. For a moment, I didn't know where I was.

The voice came again. "Shelby? Are you all right?"

I jolted into a sitting position. Austin sat beside me, my red sweatshirt zipped around his middle. He was bare-chested, his left shoulder wrapped with a dirty dressing.

"I was hoping it was all a bad dream," I said, sliding my arms around my bare legs for warmth. The morning was cool, and my ripped T and shorts felt damp from the grass beneath me. But more than that, I was sitting next to a nearly naked guy. A guy who'd been a wolf a few hours ago. Confused and embarrassed were only the basics of what I felt.

"Sorry about your jumper. I needed something to, ah, cover myself," Austin said in a weak voice.

"Don't worry about it," I said, realizing he meant my

sweatshirt. I stopped rubbing at my skin to warm myself and focused on tending Austin. I kept my eyes trained on his face and shoulder. He'd lost a lot of blood. This morning he had a pale look about him. His eyes, last night as bright as topaz, today appeared dull and dark.

"How do you feel?"

"My shoulder hurts like the blazes." He smiled, barely hiding a wince as he touched the wound.

"The fight last night? Big scary cat?"

He rubbed his head like it hurt. "Yes. I remember. All I could think was that he was going to hurt you. I couldn't let that happen."

"And you didn't."

He smiled weakly. "No, I didn't."

"I should have trusted you," I said. "I'm sorry."

"I had to earn your trust." He shrugged, wincing from the movement. "And frankly, most girls would have run away from me after what I told you."

I nodded and reached toward his dressing. We didn't have any time to waste. Austin grimaced as I pulled the cloth away from the wound. Ugh. It didn't look good.

"We need to get you some real medical help," I said, tying the makeshift bandage back in place.

"I feel fine," Austin insisted as he rose to his feet. He swayed a little, then reached out to steady himself against me. I caught him around the waist, not letting him fall. He was in much worse shape than I'd first thought.

Austin shrugged me off and tried to stand on his own again, this time successfully. "I have to get to town."

"No, we're going to camp," I said.

Austin nodded, and I saw a look of pain cross his face. "Shelby, I don't know about this. What if I change at camp?"

"Austin, you're really hurt. You need a doctor."

"But what if I—"

"Stop! I'm not going to let you die. You're bleeding badly. This is serious."

He nodded weakly. "I'm afraid," he said.

"I know, but we have to take our chances if it means you live. I'm not going to lose you. Not after . . . all this." I bit back a tear and focused on holding Austin steady.

"We can't," Austin said. "I can't let you—"

"You still think camp is this way?" I asked, pointing.

Austin nodded. "But what about Red Canyon?"

I helped Austin to his feet. "Don't worry about that."

He wrapped his right arm around me and we started walking in the direction of camp.

Sometime later, when I saw the fence, I almost keeled over with joy. But Austin and I were shuffling along at a steady pace, and keeling over with joy was pretty much out of the question. Painstakingly, we moved along through the thick brush that bordered the fence.

At last, like an answered prayer, we came to the gate. After I screamed into the intercom for help, the electric fence rattled open. Like some kind of desert wanderers, Austin and I staggered into camp.

Seconds later, Mr. Winters zoomed toward us in a golf cart. "Shelby! Are you all right? Oh, dear. Austin, what's happened? Where are your clothes?" He stomped on the brakes and nearly fell out, scrambling toward us.

"Take us to the infirmary," I said as I helped Austin into the passenger seat and then climbed into the back of the cart.

Mr. Winters hit the gas pedal and we whizzed off. We screeched to a stop in front of the infirmary. Austin moaned, holding his shoulder, and I hopped out of the backseat so I could help him out of the vehicle.

"Listen, Mr. Winters," I said, feeling that the explaining needed to happen right away. "We didn't mean to run—"

"Later," he said. "Let's take care of you kids first and then we'll talk."

"That's my camper! Oh, Austin!" Sven came running over, looking ready to hug Austin to death.

"Sven, go get some clean clothes for Austin," Mr. Winters said.

Sven ran off, and Mr. Winters and I each took one of Austin's arms and helped him up the steps of the infirmary.

The nurse, an older blond lady still rubbing sleep out of her eyes, opened the door. Her jaw dropped. "What the heck happened?" she said, taking in his condition.

"He lost his clothes in a cougar attack," I said, realizing I could tell the truth, partway at least. "He was protecting me."

Austin rolled his head toward me, a weak smile on his pale face.

"Come on, son," Mr. Winters said.

We got him into bed. Under the blankets, Austin started to shiver violently.

The nurse carefully peeled back the T-shirt fabric. "Wow. That doesn't look good." She unlocked her medicine cabinet and rummaged through it, coming up with something she injected into his arm.

"Is he going to be all right?"

"Honey, let me do my job." The nurse slipped a thermometer into Austin's mouth.

Mr. Winters caught my arm. "You need to get that looked at, Shelby."

"Huh?" I glanced down at a scratch on my arm. It was one of probably a hundred on my body from trekking through the woods. "It's from the hike."

"It could use some ointment and a bandage. Sit down." Mr. Winters pointed me to the chairs near the nurse's desk.

I kept my eyes on Austin as the nurse tended him. He'd gone very pale and his forehead was beaded with sweat. It didn't look like he was going to be out of the infirmary by tonight. What would the wolf do, injured and scared and locked in a room with the nurse?

Mr. Winters took a seat next to me and said, "I know you're worried about him." He sighed and scratched at his thinning hair. "You liked him well enough to run away with him into the woods," Mr. Winters said.

"No—that's not why we went over the fence. Charles was harassing Austin and threatening to have his dad print stuff in the tabloids."

Mr. Winters held up a hand. "Shelby, we're aware of that. After everyone noticed you two were missing, Charles slipped a message to a food delivery truck driver, promising him a reward if he'd make some calls for him. Apparently, the little turd—ahem, I mean, Charles—was trying to buy his way out of camp with tabloid headlines."

I resisted the urge to say duh. "See!"

"All famous families have to deal with the press."

"You don't understand! Charles could have ruined Austin's family."

"Charles won't be causing any more trouble," said Mr. Winters. "We sent him home this morning. But whatever he had threatened, it still doesn't excuse your running off."

"No, but Austin's different. The Bridges family is different!" Geez. How could I explain it, without explaining it? I couldn't.

He put an arm around my shoulders. "Your heart was in the right place, but you have to help yourself before you can help other people, remember? You have to take care of you."

I bit the inside of my cheek, forcing back all the frustration welling inside me. "I'm going to be sent to Red Canyon, right?"

"We don't know that for sure. We'll have to discuss it with your parents."

Even though I knew it was coming, I still shuddered at the

thought. I didn't want to spend the next two months in a desert hell. If I wasn't cut out for wimpy Camp Crescent's rules, how would I do at a place where there were more rules, military drills, and even solitary confinement?

And Austin needed me here. Even if he was going to be okay, he still didn't have his serum for next time, and for sure they'd be keeping a closer eye on him, thinking he was definitely a runner now. He had two more full moons to make it through during the camp session. But more important, what was going to happen when the moonlight streamed through the infirmary windows tonight?

Austin was still in deep trouble. And it was my fault.

If I hadn't been with him in the woods, he'd never have had that run-in with the cougar—he'd have made it to civilization and called the chemist. If I hadn't been there he'd have been home free. My hands clenched at my sides. It was my doing. My bad choice. My decision to go over the fence had brought us to this awful spot. To these consequences. I'd totally screwed up, and Austin would be paying the price.

Tonight he'd become the wolf. Tonight the world would learn the truth about the Bridges family.

I swallowed against the tight feeling in my throat. There had to be something I could do. Before I was bussed off into the Utah wastelands, I had to think of something, anything to get me closer to Austin's serum. *Which was in Mr. Winters's office. Bing. Lightbulb.*

"Um, can I call home?" I said, playing sad. "To tell them what happened. You know, to make sure they know I'm okay."

A smile brightened Mr. Winters's chubby face. "Of course! I'll walk you over there." The guy seemed to take it as some kind of a therapy victory or something. He jumped right off the chair and hurried over to his office with me.

As he unlocked the door, I said, "I'm gonna need some privacy. I've got a lot to tell my dad."

He paused. "I'll be in the hallway, then. If you need me, just holler."

Great. Well, maybe that wouldn't be far enough away for me to try to locate Austin's serum in peace, but I nodded anyway, figuring at least I'd be in his unlocked office. He dialed the phone and then handed it to me.

Priscilla answered with her typical breathless, "Hell-ooohh?"

I said, "Hello? Uh-huh. Yeah." I pretended to talk, waving Winters toward the exit. Then I smiled at him till he went out into the hall and closed the door nearly all the way.

Meanwhile, Priscilla was all "Who is this? I'm going to look you up on caller ID. Is this one of Shelby's friends? She's at camp."

I held the phone tighter. "It's me."

Priscilla paused. "Shelby? Is that you?"

Mr. Winters ducked his head around the door. "Everything all right?" he mouthed.

"Great," I said, sending him a forced smile.

"Shelby! Where are you? We've been so worried!" Priscilla babbled.

Whoa—it actually sounded like she was happy to hear from me. It was too weird and I couldn't deal, so I set the phone down. I had work to do, anyway.

"Uh-huh. Yeah. I know. Everything's fine," I said in a loud voice so Winters would think I was actually talking to and listening to Honey Bun.

I tried all the drawers of Winters's desk and went to the small closet at the back of the room. Inside was a large box, like the kind of footlocker my dad had in the basement with all his old college stuff in it. Of course, Dad's wasn't padlocked like this one. So there had to be something good in there, right? But how to get in? I mean, obviously I had to break the lock. But that would make, like, a huge noise. Winters would come running, natch.

"Shelby? Shelby?" Priscilla's voice shrieked from the phone.

"Yeah. Well, let me talk to him," I said, still playing like I was talking on the phone. I was almost out of ideas, but then I spied a camp walkie-talkie on the desk. Bingo. I clicked it on.

"Sven? Come in, Sven," I said, pinching my nose so I could imitate Cynthia Crumb's voice.

"Ya, dat's me," he came back.

"There's a golf cart crash at the front gate! Get Winters right away!" I clicked off the walkie-talkie and set it on the desk. "Uh-huh?" I said, picking up the telephone where Priscilla was squawking away in case Winters checked on me.

A second later, I heard Sven burst through the admin building's doors and shout, "You come now! Fire!" at Mr. Winters.

"I'll be back," Mr. Winters said, poking his head around the corner. "Stay here!"

I nodded, imitating a teen totally engrossed in conversation.

As soon as he was gone, I set the phone down again, then picked up the brass statue of an eagle on Mr. Winters's desk. Grunting in effort, I dragged the footlocker from the closet.

What I was about to do would be the nail in my coffin at Camp Crescent. But saving Austin was more important. I took a deep breath and made my choice. After a brief apology to the eagle, I swung at the padlocked latch on the box.

Crash! The head of the sculpture fell off and rolled under the desk, but the lock didn't budge.

"Stupid bird," I said, winding up for another swing.

Crash! I slammed the birdie down, which bent the metal holding the lock sideways. "C'mon." I bashed it with the bronze bird again. This time the padlock came loose.

I dropped the headless statue on the floor, narrowly missing my toes, and then pulled the latch and lock totally off the box. I knelt in front of the box like some kind of treasure hunter and opened it.

It was treasure, all right. Bags of chocolates, Doritos, glittery eye shadows, dirty magazines, and all kinds of other contraband filled the locker. Enough junk to supply, like, five 7-Elevens. There were also cell phones and, I recognized, my own PDA.

Nearly drunk with the smell of Hershey's Kisses and fruity gummy worms, I dug around in the stuff until I found a plastic bag buried under a stack of manga comics. Holding it up to the light, I saw the clear vials Austin needed. *Yes!*

I stuffed the plastic bag into the waistband of my shorts, along with my PDA. Then I threw the headless eagle into the footlocker. "Gotta go!" I yelled into the phone, then I hung up and ran. I only had minutes to get to Austin with the serum before they'd be back. Before they'd find out what I'd done.

"Help! Help! Flaming golf cart crash at the main gate!" I shouted as I burst into the infirmary.

"Oh, no!" The nurse grabbed a first-aid kit and then dashed out the door.

Austin moaned in his bed, turning over.

"Hey," I said, touching his cheek.

His eyelashes fluttered, then opened. "Shelby?"

"Hi. I got it for you. Do you hear me?" I said, digging the vials out.

"You have the serum? How?" Austin murmured.

"Hurry, tell me what to do!"

"Here." Austin opened his mouth wide.

I uncapped one of the tiny vials and poured the clear liquid down his throat.

He swallowed, then whispered, "Another, please."

After a glance toward the door, I uncapped a new vial and poured it in his mouth. "They'll be coming soon. I'll hide the rest of your vials in the shoes and clothes Sven brought you, okay?"

Austin nodded weakly. "Thanks," he said with a wheezing breath. His eyes closed again, and I walked over to the pile of clothes.

"Oh, one more thing," I said, looking up from stuffing his shoes with the vials. "I'm putting my PDA there, too. Keep it safe. Call someone who can help."

His eyes opened again. "Shelby?"

I moved back over to his bedside to say good-bye.

He reached out for my hand and squeezed it weakly. "I won't forget you. Ever."

My heart did a funny lurch in my chest.

Guys say that kind of forever crap all the time, but this time I believed it. Even if Austin wasn't exactly a regular guy, he still counted. In fact, he more than counted—he mattered.

Looking at him, with his damp bangs plastered to his forehead and his eyelashes quivering as he struggled to keep his eyes open, I realized how much I cared about him. In fact, I thought I could maybe love him in the right circumstances. If things were different.

I sucked in a breath, feeling sad all of a sudden, which was totally wrong—I was saving Austin and that meant I needed to be brave. "You need to get better, 'kay? Just rest," I said in my most confident voice. "I have to go now."

Austin's amber eyes looked a little glassy. "Tell them it was my fault. I broke into the office, I pinched the serum. You can't take the blame," he said sternly.

"Yes I can. This time it's all mine." I kissed him on the forehead. "Now if you'll excuse me, I have to go eat some major worms."

He gave me a funny look, because of course he didn't know I was talking about the gummy-worm stash in Winters's office.

Yeah. To distract them from what I'd actually taken, I was going to stuff myself silly.

And then turn myself in.

SIXTEEN

*M*ove it, move it, *M-OOO-VE IT!*" Sergeant Scabwell, his face red as a baboon's butt, shouted in my ear for the, like, ninetieth time that mile. "SHELBY LOCKE! ARE YOU LISTENING?"

I swayed on my feet, the heat of the afternoon getting to me. The Utah desert is not kind to fair-skinned Midwest-to-Beverly Hills transplants. After ten days at Red Canyon Ranch, I was pretty darn sure hell did exist.

"LOCKE!" shouted Scabwell again.

I lurched forward but not fast enough for the girl behind me.

Her name was Randi, a skinny kleptomaniac whose bunk was next to mine, and she picked that moment to be a freaking bulldozer. "Go, Locke!" she said, pushing with her hands.

My morale, or whatever you want to call it, was so low that I hadn't even complained about the T-shirt she'd stolen from my bag two days ago—but nobody pushes me.

"Hey!" I halted and whirled around, ready to rip her a new one.

Sergeant Scabwell popped up next to me again. "WHAT IS YOUR PROBLEM, LOCKE?" This time, little spit drops flew at me, speckling my face. Eww.

"Nothing," I said. "There is no problem."

Scabwell stepped closer, his pudgy belly making a shadow over my toes. If the dude had actually been in the army, it'd been, like, forever ago. He stuck his red pockmarked face right in mine and said, "Don't you give me any sass, Locke. Drop and give me twenty!"

"Um . . ." I glanced down at the sand around my feet, where a scorpion skittered past a pile of jagged rocks and a shriveled-up snake skin.

"LET'S GO, PRINCESS! HERE! NOW!" the sergeant yelled.

All the girls in my platoon had stopped running and were staring at me with utter disgust. Like it was my fault stupid Randi had smashed into me. It wasn't like the sergeant was making *them* do twenty.

But then Sergeant Scabwell blew his whistle and yelled, "Quit your gawking, Beta Platoon! Just for that, all of you lolly-gaggers can give me thirty!"

Grumbling, all the girls thudded to the ground and started the push-ups. Next to me, Vanessa, a heavyset black girl from Ohio, swore under her breath each time her belly hit the sand. By the time we were all done, nearly everyone was swearing at me and sweating. Like, ugly-guy sweating. Soaked T-shirts. Slimy hair. The works.

"LET'S GO, CUPCAKES!" the sergeant bellowed, smoothing the front of his green uniform. "GET ON DOWN THE TRAIL—MOVE IT!"

We slogged across more sand dunes, until finally the camp came into view, small in the distance. The huge green tents we bunked in stuck out among the Quonset buildings used for the dining hall—well, "mess hall," they called it—the administrative offices, and counselor quarters. Around all of it were miles and miles of desert surrounded by heavy-duty electric fencing that made Camp Crescent look like a bunny pen.

I totally couldn't picture Ariel here. Poor thing had really told me the truth about this place. She probably did almost die of heat exhaustion. And she didn't have this stupid rash on her arm to deal with, either. A scratch that never seemed to heal, so every time it came into contact with sand, sun, or yucky water—which was all the time—it seemed to get worse. Not the best souvenir from a trek through woods that, looking back, seemed magical.

This ugly desert had none of that magic. And it didn't even have a moon I could look at because we were into that new moon phase, where it doesn't shine for a while. The whole landscape after sundown was lit by giant spotlights from the watchtower at the front gate like we were some kind of criminals.

The platoon started down the hill toward camp, Scabwell

singing out some kind of cadence like "Sound off, one-two" and so on and on and on. I shuffled along with the rest of the inmates—I mean, campers—looking forward to the drinking fountain, a cool shower, and whatever horrible mess they'd call dinner.

Then Randi shoved me in the back again. "Look," she said, pointing down to a Jeep speeding down the rough road leading to camp. "I hope it's the mail. My grandma's sending me a new pair of flip-flops."

"What happened to the pink ones you stole from Vanessa?" I asked over my shoulder.

"Hah," Randi grunted, falling back into place.

Some kids did get care packages, but I doubted there'd be anything for me. Mail had been pretty sparse, except for a postcard from Dad the other day. He'd got my letter—the one I'd written during that Dr. Wanda session. I'd asked Ariel to mail it for me, and she had. She was a good friend, and I'd barely had a chance to say good-bye. I hoped she'd stay in touch somehow.

Dad's postcard hadn't said much more than *We'll talk when you get home*, but the *Love, Dad* he'd signed was a start, I guess.

I hadn't heard a word from Austin. That hurt the most. I was sure he'd remember I was at Red Canyon and at least write me, but maybe he was still recovering. I didn't want to think he'd forgotten all about me now that he had his serum. *Ack, just shut up and march, Shelby! Stop feeling sorry for yourself!* Getting all depressed about stuff I couldn't control wasn't going to save me from the desert.

Picking up my marching pace, I glanced over my shoulder at Randi and Vanessa, whose faces were red and sweaty. They wanted to get back to mail and showers and wouldn't think twice about stomping right over me if I fell.

We marched into camp, the kicked-up dust shimmering around us like brown mist. Another scenic afternoon at Red Canyon. Finally shuffling into Beta Platoon's tent, most of us collapsed onto our cots. Facedown on the ratty sleeping bag I'd been assigned, I was tempted to close my eyes, but if I wanted a shower, I'd best get my towel and shower shoes and get in line. But maybe one more minute in the rack. Or two . . .

"Locke!" The sergeant's crusty voice shattered the peace.

"Huh?" I rolled over. "What is it now?"

"It's called a package, princess!" he snapped, flinging it at me and then clomping off down the row of cots.

A package? I plucked it from the foot of my sleeping bag. It was a small paper-covered box that had already been opened by Red Canyon's office and then Scotch taped shut. Wait—the return address was Camp Crescent. Though I didn't dare hope the package was from Austin, my heart beat a little quicker. I ran my hand over the brown paper, not wanting to open it yet, just enjoying the feel of real mail and savoring the anticipation.

"Well?" Randi was breathing down my neck. "Aren't you going to open it?"

"Um, do you mind?" I said, hugging it to my chest.

Sighing dramatically, Randi snatched up the probably stolen copy of *People* magazine from her cot and stalked off.

I peeled back the tape and opened the box. Underneath the shredded newspaper that filled the top, I found a familiar-looking art project.

My raffia bird.

I'd never got a chance to burn it in the bonfire, to signify the birth of a new, stronger Shelby. But that was okay. Somehow I felt I'd done it. I'd made it through the forest with Austin. I'd risked myself to save him. I'd released the me that wanted to run from consequences somewhere between that night in the forest and eating my way through four packages of gummy worms.

I'd made decisions that had saved Austin. And you know what? Sometimes the price you pay for making those hard choices is totally worth it.

I turned the lopsided bird over and over in my hands, checking out my sloppy artwork, then I set it down on my sleeping bag and pulled a single sheet of folded white paper from the box.

Dear Shelby,
You are going to make it. Just remember to use your wings.
                                        Love and Light,
                                        Mr. Winters

I pressed one hand over my eyes, not wanting anyone in my platoon to see me break down, because I felt tears coming. Mr.

Winters was corny, maybe, but he kind of got me. I mean, he'd begged my dad to let me stay at Camp Crescent. That might have been okay, you know? I could see myself talking things out with Mr. Winters and it didn't seem like it'd be weird. He really did care about me. And apparently, he wanted me to make it.

My heart swelling, I folded the note back up into the perfect rectangle and placed it into the box with the bird. If Randi swiped that treasure, she was gonna be sorry.

"Hey! Are you all right, Shelby?" Vanessa asked.

"Yeah, yeah. Thanks. I'm okay." I swabbed my arm across my watery eyes, trying to suck it up and be normal.

"Sure?" Vanessa gave me a skeptical look. "Well, come on, then, or we'll miss it."

Thinking she meant the showers, I gathered up my stuff and followed her out the door. But she didn't walk toward the head, which is what they called the bathroom. Instead, she led me to a group of girls from my platoon who giggled by the corner of the mess hall.

At the front of the pack, Randi had a pair of binoculars trained on the front gate. Where she'd gotten them, I didn't even want to know. "New arrivals," she said, lowering the glasses to wink at us. "Hot ones." She handed the binoculars to Vanessa.

Vanessa whistled. "Oooh, that one in the leather jacket is fine."

"Hold up. Leather in the desert?" I said, thinking of the only person I knew who brought a leather jacket to brat camp. But it couldn't be him. Lots of kids probably have the rebel rocker streak in them, right?

"If he gets heatstroke I'll be his nurse!" Vanessa said with a hearty laugh. Randi and Vanessa slapped each other a high five.

I didn't even want to hope, but I dropped the bundle of clothes I was carrying and said, "Give me the glasses, Randi."

"Fine." She frowned at me as she handed them over. "Go for it. But I got dibs on the leather jacket guy."

I raised the binoculars to my eyes and saw one of the uniformed counselors leading a small group of boys across the main square. The blond boy in the back had a brown leather jacket over one shoulder. Not my leather jacket guy. Not by far. I let out a little sigh and moved on to scoping out the front gate and the desert road where billows of dust danced off into nothingness, just like my hope.

"See anyone you fancy?"

Huh? I swung around with the glasses, coming to rest on a sudden darkness. The darkness of a black T-shirt with yellow and red flames. Slowly, I lowered the glasses.

And found Austin in front of me.

Smiling and tan, he seemed as healthy as the first day I'd met him on that bus. "Private limo drop-off, three o'clock," he said, cocking a dark eyebrow. "Your platoon was out on a jaunt, I believe?"

The desert heat shimmied around me. This had to be a mirage or some kind of heatstroke hallucination. Was he really standing there? Man, it was hard to breathe! I managed to choke out, "What are you doing here?"

Before he could respond, I shoved the glasses in Randi's hands and told all the girls to get lost. They ran off, promising not to ever breathe a word to anyone, a code of silence that would last about five minutes.

I quickly pulled Austin to the colonel's private patio on the side of the building and jumped into his arms. It was like some kind of movie. Him swirling me around and around in a hug, narrowly missing the cactuses the colonel had planted all around his patio.

"I don't get it," I said, when my feet were back on the ground.

"I promised I wouldn't forget you," he said. "I gave my word."

The world was still spinning. I didn't know if that was from the happiness or from the swirling, but that kind of dizzy felt good. "Are you okay?" I asked. "How's your shoulder—and, you know, your little problem?"

He nodded. "I managed to phone the chemist before they took away your PDA. He pulled some strings and smoothed things out with Camp Crescent. My shoulder's healing fine."

I bit my lower lip. "Okay . . . but if things are smoothed out and everything, then what are you doing here?"

"Ah, all these questions!" Austin said, his amber eyes sparkling, like he thought it was all funny.

"Dude, you don't understand. This place is horrible. Really

horrible!" I gestured around at the colonel's so-called oasis, where the only living things besides the cactuses were the horny toads sunning themselves on some of the larger rocks. "You're a Londoner. You can't do the desert. I mean, what are they thinking sending you here?"

"Shelby, relax. It was my idea. I *asked* to come here," he said.

My mouth dropped open. "Are you *insane?*"

"Some might say so," he replied. "However, there happens to be this girl, this woman, really, I wanted to see."

I blinked at him. "You . . . came here on purpose?" I said, the words falling out of my still gaping mouth. My legs got a swoony feeling, and I seriously hoped I didn't land on a cactus if I fainted. He'd come for me? It was so stupid it was almost romantic. Unless . . .

I took a deep breath, steadying myself. "Austin, I don't need rescuing, if that's why you're here. I can take care of myself."

Austin nodded. "Of that I'm well aware. But everyone needs a little rescuing now and then."

"I don't."

Austin pulled me into his arms again. "You rescued me and you saved my life. The least I can do is help ease your suffering."

"You . . . want to ease my suffering?" I repeated, just to make sure the hot sun wasn't melting my brain. He'd come through on his promise to remember me, and now he was going to put himself through boot camp hell, too? Actually, that was pretty hot. *Oh, great. Now I'm turning red.* I patted at my burning cheeks.

"Do you think I'm the kind of guy who'd skip off into the sunset without you?"

"No. I wouldn't use the word *skip*, but—"

Austin took my hand. "My worst day with you is better than one spent alone. And," he said, "I happen to think you're worth a few hundred marches in the desert."

My gaze traveled from Austin's eyes, all golden in the sun, to his beautiful mouth. From here, his teeth looked totally safe. Safe enough to . . .

"Wait, wait," I said, pushing back from him and keeping him an arm's distance away. "You have your serum this time, right?"

"Yes, and a doctor's note," he said with a grin. "I'm to report to the infirmary at eighteen hundred hours every day."

I rolled my eyes at the stupid military time thing. It still confused me. "Well, I guess if—"

"Come here," Austin said, wrapping me in another hug. "It's so good to see you."

"You, too." It was so good to see him I felt faint. Resting my head against his strong chest, I reached up to run my hands through his hair. "They're going to cut this off, you know. They did it to this one guy whose hair was, like, down to his butt. He cried."

Austin glanced down at my forearm. "Shelby? What happened there?"

I shrugged. "Just a bad scratch."

"A scratch with puncture marks?" Frowning, he kept staring at my arm.

"Those aren't puncture marks!"

He dropped my arm, still not looking satisfied. "You ought to have the nurse look at that."

"She gave me some ointment. That's what they do even if you have a broken leg around here."

Just then, I saw movement over Austin's shoulder. Vanessa was back, hiding out behind a pair of saguaro cactuses. Well, kinda hiding out. The cactuses were pretty skinny compared to her curvy body.

"Having fun spying?" I called out.

"Randi sold you out for an extra five minutes in the shower," she said, motioning us over. "You better say your good-byes and run."

Austin slipped an arm around my shoulders and whispered, "I'll see you 'round, love. Don't worry."

He called me *love*? A smile I couldn't hold back took over my entire face while my heart did flip-flops. I gazed at him, feeling like nothing else mattered—not the boot camp, not the whole supernatural thing. It *was* the most perfect moment ever.

"Shelby! Kiss him and let's go," warned Vanessa. She put a hand on one of her thick hips and stood there watching us.

I rolled my eyes at her. "A little privacy please? I'm not going to kiss him while you're—"

Austin's lips covered mine. There in the sun-drenched court-yard, surrounded by prickly pears, sagebrush, and the most pathetic gravel work I'd ever seen, he finally kissed me. And I wasn't scared.

His lips pressed against mine, warm and lush, and his hands smoothed my hair while drawing me closer. As the kiss deepened, I breathed in the smell of his soap and skin, a combination as intoxicating as ever. I slipped deeper into his arms, wrapping my hands around his back, the feel of his T-shirt smooth beneath my fingers. Then his lips pressed slightly harder, and he teased the inside of my lower lip with his tongue. I sighed, kissing him back until I lost all sense of my surroundings. Nothing existed but me and Austin. And the kiss, which made my body tingle all the way down to my toes. . . .

The kind of kiss that certain sergeants arriving on the scene found objectionable between two reform cadets. . . .

The kind of kiss that made scrubbing burned gravy pots after dinner that night almost pleasant work. . . .

The kind of kiss that made digging a new latrine hole the next day almost fun. . . .

Then again, I figured out that really good kisses make all things bearable. Really good kisses and believing you're the kind of person you were meant to be.

And maybe, if you're lucky enough to have someone who really cares about you, someone you can trust, someone who reminds you to believe in yourself, you can survive anything— a crazy family, a forbidden forest, or even the worst desert boot camp.

Moonlight might have special powers, but love works the real magic in the world.

Only love.

ACKNOWLEDGMENTS

Special thanks to my wonderful agent, Stephen Barbara, for his encouragement and unflagging support, and to my wise editor, Anne Hoppe, for her insightful and gentle guidance.

Much love to Brenna Davis and Daryl Bunce, who welcomed me home to the city; my dear friend and writing mentor Pat White; Jen Sanders, my first new best friend in ages; Tonya Reichl, my very own Ariel; and Kevin Davis and his charming friend, Paul Walchenbach, who were a huge help. Many thanks to all of my beautifully unique family and friends—you helped me navigate through my very own, incredibly dark forbidden forest.

Thanks also to my supportive and talented critique partner, Dona Sarkar, and my YA sisters—the Buzz Girls: Stephanie Hale, Tina Ferraro, Simone Elkeles, Marley Gibson, and Tera Lynn Childs. A shout-out also goes to GSRWA, Jennifer Hoffman,

Melissa Norris, Robin Wood, and Mardi Jones, who saw me from first draft to first sale. Thank you so very much.

I will also be eternally grateful to Barb Hawkings and the amazing staff at the Concrete School District, who gave me a day job that led me to writing for teens. This was all meant to happen! And last but not least, I send my deepest appreciation to my former student Emily H. Thank you for reading my first young adult chapters, Emily . . . now go write your own.

HEATHER DAVIS

*A*t first glance, I don't seem like an outdoorsy person, but somehow I've spent a lot of time in the woods, including working as a chef in remote Alaska and teaching school in a tiny logging town in the North Cascade Mountains.

Never Cry Werewolf is an homage to both those rugged adventures and all the fun times I've spent singing stupid songs about lunch meat (eww!) and gobbling down s'mores (yum!). I didn't set out to write a book about werewolves, but I fell in love with the idea that everyone has a side of themselves that's shown to the world and one that's kept hidden.

These days, I'm enjoying big city life in the Pacific Northwest. When I'm not writing YA novels, I'm haunting my local movie theater and spending time with a colorful cast of friends and family (who do occasionally howl). You can visit me online at www.heatherdavisbooks.com.